Ali McDougal Series

Getting

Serious

By Selma Cook

The events and situations in this book were experienced by either the author herself or people who are close to the author. To protect the privacy of certain individuals, the names and identifying details have been changed.

Author: Selma Cook

ISBN 978-0-6458463-5-5 (Paperback)

ISBN 978-0-6458463-6-2 (E-book)

A Catalog record for this book is available from the National Library of Australia

Dedication

To all our young people, struggling to find their place
in the world.

CHAPTER 1

Let's be Real

This is not the story of my life. It is the story of one year of my life. From age fourteen to fifteen my life turned completely upside down. Or maybe, looking back, it actually turned right-side up.

At that time, my dad said something like, "It's time to get serious Ali!" His exact words were, "You're a (bleep) troublemaker!"

Then he announced I was being sent to Egypt. He thought he was punishing me, but he had no idea how much I missed my Aunty Nelly who had lived in Egypt, like forever. I was literally her golden-haired boy. I couldn't wait to go but I never let on. At the same time, I knew it was true. I did make trouble, mostly for myself. I was also very good at punishing my parents, although I don't know why I did that. Aunty Nelly later told me that I should become a politician because I could sell sand to the Arabs (nice one, Aunty) and because I could not only make trouble, but also capitalize on it. Maybe she's right.

To the onlooker I might look like someone who takes things in his stride. Easy-going. The thing is people have no idea what goes on inside me. A lot of the time I feel scattered. Confused. A bit impulsive. Sometimes more than a bit.

My dad had no idea. He would say in his low, gruff voice, "You have to know where you're heading in life, son."

I would nod and look like I knew what he meant, but the truth is, I didn't. And I never bothered to explain how I felt, or how difficult it was to focus at times. I didn't understand it myself. Part of me believed my dad wouldn't really care to know. But Aunty Nelly understood.

She would say, "Ach Laddie! You're an accident looking for a place to happen!"

I found comfort in the fact that she knew me and loved me anyway.

Did I mention that my family is basically Scottish? From all my family, Aunty Nelly is the one who kept her accent. It is one of the reasons I adore her!

At the best of times, - on the inside - I felt like a bundle of internal, mixed-up, competing parts all vying for my attention. There was so much going on in my head. And all that chaos inside me seemed to bubble up every now and again and show itself in outbursts of ridiculous behaviour, stubborn wilfulness, and kick-ass sarcasm. My teachers at school would look at me and scratch their heads. I was top of my class academically and usually aced the tests but – I continually heard – "Ali McDougal! Your behaviour leaves a lot to be desired" –

(mimicking authoritarian voice!) It was like a broken record. I felt sorry for my teachers. But I consoled myself that they were getting paid to deal with me. Yeah, I made them work for it. Don't misunderstand me, there is also a lot of compassion inside of me but that is something that someone my age would never admit. It was like I had to be 'the man' and that meant tough and confident. I tried, but I'll let you in on a little secret – I'm scared a lot of the time, unless I enter my 'inner scattered zone'. That's the part inside me that only sees hair-brain opportunities, and consequences just don't exist. So, compassion, alongside all the other random bits and pieces that make up who I am, all gets stacked away inside me, and they pop up and take over when the opportunity arises. Maybe that's where this little voice inside me comes from. But more about that later.

Mum has a voice like honey and when she praises me, I just melt and feel like a king. I haven't heard her praising me for a while though. My mum used to say that I'm a "stable fellow". I think she had read a book about positive psychology and was expressing to me what she wanted me to be, rather than what I actually was. Good try Mum! She was always hopeful. Although I must say I rarely missed Friday *Jumaah* at the *masjid*, and I'm pretty good at keeping up with my prayers. And I have *never ever* missed a basketball match! If I do all that, and keep up my good marks at school, mum is happy. She turns a blind eye to the video games and meaningless internet chat and occasional mindless pranks. My dad, however, is another story.

It is hard to ignore my dad. He's just over six feet tall, broad, and strong with a booming voice. He can't whisper! Everything about him is loud, big, and confrontational. He is the original 'tough guy'. Even his stony silences are deafening. When I was fourteen – before I was sent to Egypt – if I stood on tippy toes, I would reach my father's chest. I don't think I'll ever be as tall or as physically strong as him, but now, years later, I don't really care. I mean, I've learned that strength is not just in your muscles; it comes from somewhere deep inside and makes your body do what your mind tells it. That's an Aunty Nelly quote!

I have a good memory and I think I remember most

of the things my Aunty Nelly ever told me. And more than that, I remember how she could make me feel sorry even before I realized I'd done something wrong. She's nothing like her brother – my father – she's five foot nothing, quite ordinary. She doesn't stand out in a crowd, but I can recognize her footsteps and I know when she means business. Everything about her emanates energy. Some kind of wakefulness and awareness.

"She's switched on," I used to tell my friends.

At first, I told them as a kind of warning to watch out. Later, after that eventful year in Egypt had passed, my words glowed with pride.

"My Aunty Nelly is switched on!"

So, if Aunty Nelly is switched on, then my dad is switched off. Especially when it comes to me. He hardly looks up from his books, especially when I'm in the room. I'll admit that it hurt me that he didn't acknowledge or appreciate my going to the *masjid* without being asked, or my A on a maths test, or even excellent academic reports from school.

"That's what you're supposed to do," he would say in his rough, raspy voice.

But I would get plenty of attention whenever I

'messed up', which was often. So, I would tell myself 'I'm not good enough'; 'I'm a troublemaker'. Perhaps it was those thoughts that made me give up trying to please him and work hard to prove him right.

I maintained my A student status but supplemented it with being the class clown. I would go to the *masjid* but I would also glue myself to video games and social media. I can't remember the first day when I started talking back to mum and ignoring dad like he ignored me. I stopped being mum's angel and started being a 'royal pain in the neck' (that's a 'dad' quote).

I admit, my parents were exasperated. And they did try their best to shape me in a good way. But the events during that year from fourteen to fifteen shaped me in a way my parents never could. The best thing Mum and Dad ever did was pack me off to Egypt to Aunt Nelly's place in Cairo. She was the one who put me on the right track. It all started the night I scored the winning goal.

CHAPTER 2

A Goal-After All

Who would have thought that something as trivial as this would end up like it did? I just don't get it. I'm not all bad. But this basketball match was to become the proverbial 'last straw' for my parents – the straw that broke the camel's back. This is how it went down.

I heard the crowd cheering like crazy and I was loving it! My coach was yelling at me – nothing unusual about that.

I heard him shout, "Go! Go! Go!"

My ears were filled with the sound of me pounding down the court. Crowd roaring. As I recall, after it was all over, no one noticed how my ball handling had improved. No one saw my drive to the basket and that sick dunk I made! There's nothing like being cheered on. I was on fire!

Okay, I know I made a mistake, but it isn't the end of the world! Isn't everyone allowed one mistake, at least once, without all the fuss?

I could argue that I did score the winning goal. I was concentrating like they'd always told me to. I was focused on the game, running for my life to get the goal and win the match for the tournament – and I did. I dunked a beauty in the other team's goal, and they won the match.

My coach was actually shouting, "No! No! No!" Isn't it human error that I heard "Go! Go! Go!"?

But all was not lost. They did carry me on their shoulders amid hoots and cheers and yeah, I liked that. Good to be a hero, but of course my dad, my coach and my team didn't see it that way. Whatever! At that moment, I really didn't care.

This is what my dad said, "Irresponsible, fool-headed, smarty-pants (that's the polite term), troublemaker, too good for yourself, can't tell right from wrong, never admit you're wrong."

I can't remember much more, it's all a blurred jumble of adjectives.

I thought – I really thought – that would be the end of it. A bit of a rant and rave and then, peace. But their final decision was to ship me off to Egypt! Of all places! I know that my grandmother had lived there years ago and there are lots of family stories but, why Egypt? I knew I would be staying with Aunty Nelly – and I loved that idea – but I wanted them to feel bad, so I said, "I feel like a Chechnyan during Stalin's purges being sent to Siberia!" (Yeah, I like to read.) At least that is how I described my feelings to my mum. She likes to talk about feelings. And do you know what she said?

"Don't be ridiculous honey. Siberia is really cold, and Egypt is hot. Have you packed your sunscreen?" Looks like I'm going.

CHAPTER 3

At the Airport

"Well, it's a good day to leave Australia," I mumbled. The patches of fog made me forget glorious days at the beach, my friends, fun, freedom. Dad heard me and gazed up at the dark, grey sky.

"Yeah," he said, purposely looking away from me.

"With any luck Dad, the plane will fly off course and I'll end up in Bali! I'll send you a post card."

I faked a smile, determined to be smug. My eyes zoomed in on mum's handbag. She had promised to give me money.

"Oh yes honey," she fumbled in her bag. "I wanted to give you something."

My eyes widened hopefully. Some cash would be nice.

She reached into her bag and took out a huge book. The latest novel? She smiled and handed it to me and gave me a little pat on the arm.

"Here's a little something to read on the plane," she said well-meaningly.

"Oh great," I said with great sarcasm. "I've been looking for a good book on child abuse laws in Australia!" My voice intensifying with every word.

People started to turn toward us and stare. I looked at my parents, only Dad looked me in the eye.

"You are sending me to a third world country you know. Poverty, disease – I'll probably end up needing counselling for years!"

I was challenging him. But then I was always challenging him.

I waited for a response. Nothing.

"And you'll have to pay for it!" I added, pointing a bony finger.

Silence.

I looked at mum's hijab resting untidily on her head, covering her dark blonde hair. It never did look quite right. She averted my gaze and stared out the window at planes taking off. She discreetly wiped a stray tear with the corner of her scarf. Dad looked like he'd aged in the past few weeks. He wasn't as angry as usual. Bits of grey were shining from his once reddish blonde mop of curls. Had I done that? Was I responsible for those grey hairs? I'm not going to think about that now.

At last, he croaked, "It'll be a good experience for you son. It'll be the making of you."

There was emotion in his voice. His voice was starting to break. Was he changing his mind?

"YOLO," I said, feet apart to solidify my stance. Arms crossed in front of me, cap on backwards (just to irk my dad) and staring straight ahead. "It'll be great. Can't wait," I half-lied. "I hope Aunty Nelly has saddled the camel, all ready to go."

I could feel an explosive sarcastic episode coming on. Dad cut it short.

"Now don't go making trouble for your aunty, she's got a lot on her plate and it's very good of her to take 'you' on," he said more sternly.

He stood straighter, put his shoulders back and faced me. He towered over me. I felt helpless. Hopeless. That moment of compassion for me had fizzled out.

Nelly was his favourite sister. They had both been born in Scotland and had migrated with their mother when they were young. Nelly had married and left for Egypt years before. Her husband had died way back, but she stayed on in Cairo. She never had kids. Maybe that's why she adores me so much.

"Oh, don't worry Dad. Aunty Nelly and I go way back. Remember, I'm her number one golden-haired boy." I couldn't help but smile at the memory.

Every memory I have of Aunty Nelly is a good one. Her visits were marked by chocolate crackles on the sly, trips to the zoo, funny stories, and lots of hugs. Even when I was pint-sized, I was still taller than her. "She will have to speak through a loudspeaker if she wants me to hear her now," I thought.

"Ach aye!" I mimicked. "I'll drag that Scottish blood out of the wee pet, don't ye worry, he'll be grrrand."

I thought I had imitated my Aunty very well. My parents just looked at me, then at each other. Then they started chuckling. This was a rare occasion.

My dad didn't usually chuckle. Long ago, Dad had dropped most of his Scottish accent. Mum – an Aussie through and through – appreciated the long, rolling rrrrs.

Me! The golden-haired boy! Did I mention I have bright red hair? "Maybe Egypt won't be so bad after all," I thought.

CHAPTER 4

Aunty Nelly

"Aunty! You've changed!" I commented abruptly.

The camel (I'd imagined) had been replaced with a shiny, red Fiat. I threw my bag onto the back seat and climbed in the front.

"*Salam Alaikum Pet.*"

She leaned over and gave me a peck on the cheek as if she'd seen me yesterday – not a few years ago.

I leaned in, ready for a hug but it never came. She looked me up and down as we sat in the airport traffic and her gaze lingered as she took in my mass of bright red curls, pushed to the back of my head by a head band. Blue today. My hair was my trademark, my pride and joy.

"That will have to go," she said curtly, pointing at my head with a short stubby finger.

"I can't survive without my head Aunty!" I laughed.

I didn't want to think about what she really meant. I started to laugh – at nothing. I was desperate to change the subject.

"Anything! But not my hair," I thought.

"Don't be daft Laddie," she said calmly. "Your currrrls! You'll stop the traffic looking like that."

My curls!

"That's not going to happen Aunty," I said as gently and politely as I could.

"Hmmm," was all she said. War had been waged. Was this our first – of many – battles?

Where was my doting, kind, funny aunty of yester-year? Who was this person?

It didn't take long before I realized there was a conspiracy going on – against me! My woes had followed me halfway around the world. Dad just wouldn't let things lie. Now Aunty Nelly knew about me wagging school, my 'bold, disrespectful manner' (that's how the principal of my old school described it), walking out of class and my prowess on the basketball court. I was determined to keep my head held high and maintain my dignity. Hopefully, she wouldn't remember about my currrls.

"So, Aunty, when do I start school?" I asked one blistering, hot morning, while I shoved eggs, cheese and whatever I could get my hands onto into my mouth.

"I love the food in Egypt. Really tasty," I smiled.

I'd heard about schools in Egypt; very strict, no monkey business. I was determined to give it all a miss by using psychology – yes, I do like to read. I thought it might just work to bring the subject up myself then work my way around it. Aunty looked me over. I started to recognize that look. I called it the Sergeant Major Stare (SMS for short). It was inevitably followed by a comment, a command, a piece of advice or all three.

I tried to talk Aunty out of her SMS, but she was

rock solid; focused on me.

"School has started for everyone else but you, Love."

"Love?" I thought. Am I hearing her right? Maybe things are looking up. Afterall, 'Love' is an endearing term.

"Go on Aunty. Tell me more. Don't make me beg," I said with growing interest.

My heart was beating about to pop out of my chest and my stomach was tied in knots a sailor would be unable to undo. I tried to make my bluey-green eyes as shiny as I could, as I blinked innocently, looking up at her expectantly. (I was sitting down at the time and Aunty was standing up). All those days wagging school, escaping from....well, school. But if I didn't have to go to school here, what could I possibly turn my many talents to?

"And wipe that silly look off yer face Laddie."

I stopped in my tracks. I was amazed. Twice as big as her and ten times stronger yet I could do nothing else but obey. Now that is power.

"Ye'll not be going to school Ali McDougal."

Did she think that was a punishment?

"I love you Aunty," I cried out, jumping up from the table and leaping over to embrace her in a bear hug. Her feet were off the floor.

"Put me down young man!" she squeaked.

I placed her gently onto her wooden stool and looked at her with love. Could this be true? No school? I was afraid to find out.

"Do ye like horses Laddie?"

"Aye I do."

She raised an eyebrow. "Don't be cheeky young man."

"Yes, Aunty I like horses."

Like horses? I love horses. The only thing better than playing basketball was galloping bareback along the beach on a fast horse. I shook my head with amazement and sheer happiness.

"Am I to ride Aunty?"

"Well, your father's sent me money for your education and I'm to spend it as I see fit."

Things were obviously getting better. I could feel it. I couldn't help it – I started to do a victory dance right then and there in the kitchen. Feeling sure of myself, I thought that it might take time and a lot of effort but maybe, just maybe, I could eventually twist Aunty around my little finger. That's when I started to take notice of the little voice inside me that had nearly gone hoarse trying to get my attention for ages. The voice from deep within my psyche told me 'Don't be stupid! She's a million miles ahead of you!'

"And don't think you'll have a say in the matter you young scoundrel. I'm three steps ahead of ye."

The smile faded on my face and my fancy footwork came to a screeching halt.

"But Aunty you said horses, and that has to be good, right?"

"Aye Pet, it will be good, *inshallah*." She was softening a little. "Ach Laddie, you're such a baby."

I ignored 'the baby' comment.

"So, tell me more," I urged her in my wide-eyed meekest voice.

"You'll be learning dressage and later on, showjumping, *inshallah*, at the best government stables in Cairo with General Ghuraab – an ex-army officer."

I blurted out, "Am I to join the army? The Egyptian army? No way!"

I was backing off, heading toward the door. Boot

camp! Long treks through the desert. Not me!

"I'm going to the Australian embassy Aunty – that's too much. I'm not going!" I actually stamped my feet.

"You're not listening Love! Calm down. He's a retired general and he'll teach ye many things. And, no, you won't have to join the army, although it's not such a bad idea."

My mind was still buzzing. A general – retired – old – grumpy – used to being obeyed unquestioningly. Oh no!

CHAPTER 5

General Ghuraab

Crow. That's what Ghuraab means. I stared at the daunting figure of a huge man with crisp, grey hair. He was wearing knee-length khaki shorts, a long sleeve khaki jumper, knee-high socks, and boots that looked like they were designed to kick down a tank. He trudged around the dusty arena, barking out commands. There was no humour in his face. No softness.

"So, he's the one who is supposed to make a man out of me." I scowled as I muttered under my breath. My knees shook.

As it turned out he and I didn't start off on the right foot. It began something like this.

※

I was riding the most beautiful black Arabian horse called *Ra'd* (meaning Thunder). Now *Ra'd* had an attitude problem. He must have known what his name meant because just looking at him made me shake a little in my brand-new riding boots. Yes, I know, a far cry from barefoot, bareback horse riding at the beach. And I had to wear a helmet and – excuse me – jodhpurs! The only comfort was that my friends back in Australia would never see me. My Aussie mates and I used to hire horses; fast hacks, trained and eager, then take off racing along the beach and over sand dunes. This was completely different. I'd heard enough about the temperamental nature of Arabian horses, and I was secretly apprehensive – maybe this was beyond me? I had a feeling that I was no match for *Ra'd* or even the General for that matter. I didn't know what to expect.

Ra'd actually looked at me out of the corner of his eye. I'm sure of it! He had it in for me! But not being one to give up, I pushed my curls to the back, made a ponytail and popped my helmet on.

"Let's just see how this all plays out," I thought. I was full of hope.

My mind was racing. My thoughts were exploding. I was entering the 'scattered zone' within myself. A place of endless opportunities and no consequences in sight.

I entered the ring on *Ra'd* at a gentle walk. So far, so good. There were five other riders all about my age. Stony faced and obedient. I started to feel a bit more confident. I could do this. What a boring bunch!

The General was standing in the middle of the ring like a circus ringmaster, stock whip in hand.

"Hmm, wonder what that's for?" I thought, looking at the whip.

He cracked the whip, which made me jump a little in the saddle. *Ra'd* didn't even flinch.

It was hard to tell how old General Ghuraab was. His hair was short, his beard was snow white, his body was all muscle, and he was at least six foot three inches, or so. His face was a mass of lines and creases. He didn't look happy often but when he did, his head went back, and he roared with laughter from the depths of his soul.

The rest of the time he kept a critical eye on everything and everyone around him. Most things – and people – met with his disapproval which was hard to ignore. People tiptoed around him. I didn't know all this when I entered the dressage ring.

The General started bellowing out orders to poorly clad, cowered young soldiers who jumped when they heard his commands. They ushered the riders in and closed the gates.

"I'm not going to jump. I won't flinch! Not me!" I thought stubbornly.

In retrospect, I must have looked a fright with my bright, red mass of curls trying to escape from under my riding helmet. In the hot Egyptian sun, I had quickly turned into one big freckle even though I plastered sunscreen all over. Today I had completed the plastering with green zinc cream over my nose – to match my eyes!

I thought I looked like a work of art. Later Aunty would comment when she saw that my helmet had pushed my frizzed-out curls down, forming a circle around my neck.

"Ye look like yer' halo has slipped and is choking ye!" She had laughed – a lot.

One of the first things I learnt about the General was his ability to shout loud enough to pop your eardrums one minute and the next minute laugh – a grand belly laugh - that made his students – except me – relax a little.

I felt like I was floating in the air when I rode *Ra'd*. He glided across the turf like a ship on a calm sea. Or maybe, a ship in the desert. How poetic I am! I didn't have to do anything really except sit there – properly!

The other riders sat without any expression on their faces. They didn't look like they were having much fun and I was determined to have fun. But after I'd been around the circle several times, I started feeling a bit bored. I could see Aunty Nelly in the distance sitting under a beautiful flowering tree. Its bright red flowers cascaded around her, forming nature's red carpet for amazing people. Her *hijab* was flowing in the gentle breeze. She was drinking tea and focused intensely on reading her book.

"I wonder what she's reading?" I thought. What is it about my family and books? Anyway, the General had left the circle momentarily, and horses and riders continued the drill; back straight, head up, shoulders back, heels down, hands relaxed. The old General had disappeared into a building, but I could still hear his barking orders echoing in my ears, "Ali! Feet! Ali! Shoulders! Ali! Hands! Ali! Ali! Ali!"

Maybe he just liked my name. Well, minutes passed and there was no sign of the old fellow, so I started thinking. Aunty wasn't within earshot and even if she called out to me from where she was, I could pretend I didn't hear; you know my hair and helmet were covering my ears.

It all happened without a plan. No strategy. No goal. First, I laid my right leg across the saddle, slouched over, then leaned back, hands cradling the back of my head like I was in a cowboy film. I imagined I was chewing on a length of straw. That was fun. So far *Ra'd* kept to his steady gait around the circle. Then I crouched down with my feet on the saddle (instead of in the stirrups) and my arms spread out. I thought I was pretty good actually.

Never overbalanced! Not even once! I could see the other riders taking an interest, despite themselves, so I moved on to the grand finale.

I slowly turned around in the saddle, careful where I put my feet – a little bit at a time – until I was facing the back of the horse, still crouched down with my arms outstretched. I closed my eyes. The perfume from the trees filled my senses, the cool morning breeze stroked my face. Slowly, I stood up, my arms still outstretched. It was about 6.30 am. I imagined I was flying. I was in that scattered zone again and loving it! So many opportunities! No consequences?

"Ali McDougal! What the (something in Arabic) are you doing boy?"

Intuitively, I dropped to the saddle with a bump, sitting awkwardly with my arms still outstretched. I opened my eyes and smiled. I couldn't help it really. I don't think the General had ever seen a circus performer before in his dressage ring. I was glad to be the first. The thing is, I felt a bit awkward. Almost trapped.

"Ah yes Ali," he said as he approached, smacking his whip against his huge thigh. He spoke perfect English.

"I heard that you can't tell one end of a basketball court from another, but I would have thought a horse would be easier for you to decipher."

He got me there. He didn't have to bring up my mistake in front of all these people. My faced glowed red; well even more red that usual. My pride had suffered a distinct injury. I was determined not to change my position – facing the horse's rear end – even though I could no longer feel my legs. I felt a bit uncomfortable with my arms outstretched so I slowly brought them to my sides, never once taking my eyes off the old General. It was man against almost-man. I was doomed.

"So, Ali McDougal, you think you can ride, eh?"

"I know I can," I found myself saying. That small voice from deep within shouted, "Just be quiet!'

"Interesting," was all the General said.

He walked, or rather marched nearer to *Ra'd*, extended his massive hand and promptly gave the horse a mighty smack on the rump. *Ra'd* jumped up a bit then broke into a canter. I must say in my defence that I managed to keep my seat for about eight seconds. That would have been a success in the rodeo circuit. Maybe I should join a rodeo? Then I felt like I was flying because I actually was. It felt nice – really nice – til I hit the turf, landing fair and square on my rear end. *Ra'd* stopped, turned and looked at me, then snorted. That is horse for '*gotcha* fool!' All the other horses and riders had now stopped. Their carefully timed gait interrupted. All faces were turned toward me, laughing. Hoots of laughter were punctuated by Arabic words flying like dark arrows towards my bruised rear end and my battered pride.

Part of me felt like a hero – I ignored the other part. I sat on the turf not wanting to get up just yet. The thumping pain in my rear end didn't help. The General – the only one who hadn't laughed – approached and said more quietly.

"Now, Ali McDougal, if you'd been facing the head of the horse, instead of its rear end, and sitting correctly, you wouldn't have fallen off. Hmm?"

I knew he was right. He extended his hand, the same one that had slapped *Ra'd*. I hesitated. I knew that in the world of Ali McDougal this should mean war. But as I looked the General in the eye and saw a faint twinkle and the broad hand ready to help, I knew I'd just made a friend. So, I smiled. A big cheesy grin and took hold of his hand. He pulled me up as if I were a mosquito. Pretty good for an old fellow.

"Get back on the horse, Ali! Now!"

The brief amiable interlude was over. He was shouting commands again. I stumbled over to *Ra'd*, patted his neck with a gesture of apology and climbed back into the saddle, sitting carefully this time; the thumping pain reminding me of what had just passed. The rest of the session and the hundreds that followed were all a bit of a blur. After six months of six mornings a week and three hours at a time, I thought I was ready for the Olympics. When I brought up the subject to the General one morning as we strolled across the field towards the café, I mentioned the Olympics in passing with a bit of a nod and a smile. He didn't say yes but he also didn't say no. That was good enough for me.

Years later I recalled those glorious mornings in the heat and flies of Cairo, and the fields dotted with majestic Arabian horses of all colours and sizes. I closed my eyes and remembered the smell of hay, the perfume of trees, the buzzing of bees and the sound of my boots clacking excitedly to the stables. I also recollected the mantra of the General spoken in his husky, heavily accented voice, "Just do what you are supposed to do Ali, and do it well."

CHAPTER 6

Cairo

Initially, I was a bit overwhelmed in Egypt. Part of
it was seeing how Aunty Nelly had changed towards me.
Or was it me who had changed? I wanted to spend time
with Aunty, but I didn't like the fact that I *had* to be here.

I don't like being forced to do anything. Anyway,
in conceding defeat to the fact that I would have to spend
at least one year of my life in Egypt, I finally decided to
make the best of it, thinking that my parents would be

none the wiser. Why didn't I want them to know I was changing?

I visited the Pyramids in Giza, sailed on a *falukha* on the Nile River, watched dancing horses and ate my fair share of *falafel* (known locally as *taa'maya*), *ful* beans and *kofta*. The crowded streets and marketplaces were all a novelty at first and I relished the excitement, the change. I even got to play basketball at Zuhoor Sporting Club in Nasr City (*Nadi Zuhoor*) where Aunty was a member. I charmed the coach and my team members with my red hair, freckles, and broad smile. A foreigner, I was a novelty to the other boys and the people I met generally. It was nice to be the centre of attention, without the recriminations from back home in Australia. I never repeated the mistake I had made on the basketball court and always dunked the ball in the right net! I enjoyed the fact that my newfound friends knew nothing about my inglorious past.

Gradually, I got to see the other sides of Cairo. There are certainly more than two sides. Aunty tried to keep me firmly within her circle of *masjid*-going people and I must admit that I loved the echoing call of the *adhan* in the early morning when the air was cool. I relished walking to the nearby *masjid*, listening to the birds with the hum of traffic always in the background. I must admit that in such an environment, I managed to keep up my daily prayers; even better than I had in Australia. And I learned more *Quran* too. I was on a roll!

Aunty took hold of the reins of my education and apart from six mornings a week with the General, she insisted on home schooling me. I called it home drilling. It lasted four hours a day except Friday. Aunty hardly let me lift my head from my books. I will never complain about Australian schools ever again!

She taught me grammar, writing techniques, poetry, the classics, geography, and history. I always had a book with me that I was supposed to read by a certain time. I knew I would be questioned and questioned again. That I would have to explain back to her what I'd learnt, adding why I thought it was interesting, important, or not. There was nothing I could venture to say without her asking me 'why?' She left no stone unturned, no meaningful phrase unexplained. She was my tormentor. But more than all the work and study, she taught me discipline. How to finish a task. How to organize my time. And she did it without raising her voice or making empty threats. All she had to do was raise that uncanny eyebrow and give me an SMS and I was back in line. She made me feel helpless! I don't even know why I listened and obeyed, but I did.

I also had a teacher come in and teach me maths and science and another one for Arabic and Quran.

"Not my forte Laddie," she had said and that was that.

My days were filled with learning, horses, basketball, *masjids* and Aunty.

She had insisted that before I arrived in Cairo, she had no white hair, but I begged to differ and did her the honour of counting them for her every day before we started our classes. I loved her. I feared her; I feared losing her love, and moreover, her respect.

If I worked to her satisfaction, she'd let me attend basketball training which took place in open-air courts in the scorching sun of summer or the piercing winds of winter. I learned the meaning of tough and there was no anger or aggression in it. Even in Ramadan, my Egyptian mates and I would play basketball in the searing heat while we were fasting. We never complained. We would get bottles of cool water and pour them over our heads and continue playing. In my early days in Cairo it was summer, so complete with sunhat and zinc cream I ran and dribbled and dunked and defended and all the while I was learning Arabic: ball, match, go, stop, no!, what are you doing? Come back! Again. Again. Again.

The coaches only spoke Arabic but most of the boys went to international schools and could speak English. I was living the life. I came to understand that my teammates and I were considered 'elite' in Egyptian society because we had money, opportunity, and education. My family is not wealthy, but being a foreigner meant I jumped the queue and became an honorary member of 'the elite'. I was looking at the whole picture of Egypt through, not only the eyes of a Muslim, but through the eyes of an Australian Muslim.

The idea that everyone should have a 'fair go' had been drilled into me since I was little. I'd seen a lot of poverty; the City of the Dead, child labourers, beggars and corrupt police. A part of me felt ashamed. I knew I was not elite at all. Why couldn't that little kid, who was carrying bricks, come and play basketball? When I mentioned this to my teammates they laughed scornfully and made fun of the boy. They might give him some money – a few Egyptian pounds - as charity, but not one of them was willing to share their life.

I started to feel different from the rest of them. That voice inside me was constantly nagging, "What makes them think they're any better than that little Egyptian boy carrying bricks?" And, "You know better, don't forget it." For once, my little voice and I teamed up.

CHAPTER 7

A *Wee Thing*

Aunty Nelly had focused her mind, her energy, and her waking hours on me. She was committed. All the sweets, stories, and hugs of my younger years when she used to visit us in Australia, didn't prove her love for me as much as her sitting next to me day after day. She showed up! Everyday. She persevered until I could write a well-balanced essay, articulate properly, and tell her the countries and capital cities of the world as well as discuss the latest politics. She drove me around, waited for me, watched me, and told me off when required. I saw her power, determination and will, and I felt her love.

Even after a few months in Egypt I hadn't really seen Aunty interacting with everyday Egyptians. Shopping was something she liked to do without me. She said she spent much more money when I was with her. Anyway, I didn't mind staying home usually, but then, one day, I was in a bad mood. I don't know why. It might have been the weather (it was dusty), the flies (there were billions of them!), lack of sleep (I'd had tons of studying to do) or perhaps it was me – the almost-man, Ali – wanting to assert himself. Yeah, that was probably it. Maybe I wanted to show Aunty that I was the man of the house. It must have been a deep, subconscious, primordial thing. Perhaps I'll never know. That little voice inside me was rolling its eyes and saying, "Oh! Here we go again!"

So, anyway, I went shopping that day with Aunty and yes, she spent loads more money buying ice cream, cakes and whatever I could beg from her.

Then on the way home, I pleaded for some '*Abu*

Mazen'! This is a semi-outdoor *shawarma* shop that sells the best, and I mean the best *shawarma* you could ever have. *Shawarma* is like a souvlaki or a kebab, only better! It makes the ones they make in Australia taste like a cheap imitation.

On that day, I saw another side of Aunty Nelly. A side that relegated her to hero status in my eyes. This is what happened.

I must admit that when we approached the shop to order our *shawarmas,* all I could think of was my stomach. The almost-man inside me was starving. I was mesmerized as I watched the vertical rotisseries; one with chicken and one with lamb slowly orbiting the heating element. My eyes glazed over. The smell of spices filled the air. I was in heaven! I was so enthralled that I didn't notice the drama that was unfolding just a short distance from where I stood.

One of the things I learned in Egypt was that - generally speaking - the police are the bad guys. Not to say that the robbers are the good guys. It's just that the system had given the police a lot of unregulated powers and many took advantage of that.

The *shawarma* shop was just to the side of a

building's entrance and apparently the 'burly police officer' who instigated the one-sided fight that day had met the shop owner before. There was some disagreement about where exactly the cash register table should be. Burly Police Officer was insisting that the table be moved two or three centimetres to the left. Shop Owner, however, condemned himself to cruel and unusual punishment that day by saying, "There is plenty of space. A few centimetres won't make any difference."

He said it so quietly that I didn't hear him. Aunty told me all about it afterwards. As soon as those words were uttered, Burly Police Officer lunged at him and started punching the living daylights out of him. Shop Owner knew better than to fight back and no one in the shop or on the street came to the rescue. No one said a word. No one even looked. People completely ignored what was happening.

My attention was plucked from the spicy chicken *shawarma* I'd just ordered when I heard a loud crash, bang, and painful groan. Burly Police Officer was at least three times bigger and stronger than Shop Owner who never resisted. The almost-man inside me stared in amazement, stuck in one place. I froze. I had never seen violence like this, except in a movie or a video game. This was real.

I glanced down at Aunty Nelly and immediately saw the SMS glare. It was turned on full force. It wasn't even directed at me, but I had the feeling I'd done something wrong! Before I could collect myself, Aunty Nelly walked straight over to Burly Police Officer and stared him down with her SMS stare. She never moved her eyes from his face. He interrupted his pounding on Shop Owner's helpless body to see who was invading his sanctum. When his eyes met Aunty's, she started! She began reciting *"La hawla wa la quwatta illah billah"* over and over with a distinct Scottish twang. It sounded rather nice, but I still stared in horror.

The almost-man inside of me was horrified that I might have to take on Burly Police Officer and defend Aunty. It started to back-off and disappear somewhere in the depths of my petrified psyche. Would I have to intervene? Man of the house? Me? I felt helpless. Not good. My mind went blank. I remained riveted in my place. I followed Aunty's movements with stoic concentration. The thing is, she showed absolutely no fear while I was drowning in it! If I had been Burly

Police Officer, I would know that I had to stop whatever I was doing. As I watched her, I was learning the power of courage!

Putting things in context, it is important to realize that Aunty had two distinct advantages that enabled her to step up, when so many others didn't. One, she is white, and two, she is a woman and those things combined, gave her a degree of immunity and she knew it. She had simply decided to turn them to Shop Owner's advantage. In so doing, she managed to turn white privilege on its head!

I watched. I waited. I was anticipating another level of disaster. But she continued reciting the same Arabic words slowly, clearly, methodically. Then I noticed a look of fear on Burly Police Officer, and he started scrambling. He kept looking from one side to another. He was clearly uncomfortable. Not as uncomfortable, however, as beaten-up Shop Owner. But Burly Police Officer's sense of entitlement was quickly melting away.

Nevertheless, he picked up Shop Owner and pushed him inside the entrance to the building. He was like a Rottweiler toying with a rag doll.

The truth is, he was trying to get away from Aunty! A

wave of relief came over me. Aunty's safety meant I didn't have to intervene!

But then I saw her follow him into the building! My heart was racing again. She was still reciting those words but louder and firmer. Burly Police Officer stopped pounding Shop Owner, then threw him against the wall – hard. Then, muttering something in angry Arabic, he left the building. As a Muslim, he knew the meaning of those words – he backed off. As soon as he disappeared, the workers in the *shawarma* shop came bounding to Shop Owner's rescue. They picked him up and carried him to a tap and washed him down. Someone called for a doctor. There is usually a doctor in the streets somewhere. One arrived on the scene. After a very short time, things went back to normal. Aunty returned to my side. I looked at her and shook my head. Was it all a dream?

"Are the *shawarmas* ready yet Laddie?" she asked, as if nothing had happened.

"S*hawarmas?* Who cares about *shawarmas,* Aunty! What just happened over there? I thought you might die today!"

"Ach it's just a wee thing." She paused, then looked up at me and said, "Sometimes you just have to do whatever you can to make things right."

I looked down at Aunty. My tiny, pint-sized hero. She was like David taking on Goliath! Only she hit him with words, not a sling shot. I admired her presence of mind and her absolute fearlessness in the face of potential catastrophe.

She was watching me as I struggled to process my thoughts. That little voice inside me was cheering her on; lost for words.

"Aunty," I said in a half-whisper. We were still waiting for our *shawarmas*. "I think this is the end for Shop Owner."

I pointed at the deserted cash register table. "Burly Police Officer will probably come back later," I added.

I felt worried.

"Ach Laddie! The story doesn't end. It just changes. Perhaps something changed today. Even a *wee* bit."

I was sure of that.

CHAPTER 8

Underdog

I had a problem. Aunty didn't really like one of my friends. His name was Hany. Now Hany and I had quite a bit in common. Perhaps that's what worried her. He wasn't one of the well-off boys that went to the Club to play basketball. He was a poor boy who worked to help support his family. I had met him when he was delivering groceries for a small supermarket down our street. He spoke some English and I entertained him with my attempts at Arabic. But Aunty was concerned.

"That boy's got a look," she would say, seemingly indifferent.

"A look?" I echoed. "Aunty! You're the queen when it comes to giving looks. You could stop a buffalo with your SMS glare!"

I couldn't get the image of Burly Police Officer out of my mind.

"Hmm I don't like that boy," she repeated.

"You can't just not like him Aunty. He's my mate. My Egyptian mate! I'm going out with him on Friday night."

I knew I was challenging her. The little voice within me just shook its head.

"Are you asking me or telling me young man?" She turned and stood as straight and tall as she could.

"Arr asking?"

"No!" she answered.

"Why?"

"I told ye I dunna like the boy."

"It's *haram* to judge people without evidence," I said, thinking how brilliant I was. It worked. She stopped what she was doing and thought for a while. I took my chance and added, "He's just invited me to meet his family and have dinner at his house."

I tried not to make my eyes look too wide and innocent because she would never believe me.

"I don't know his family, Ali," she said, still a bit uncertain.

But I could tell she was in the process of changing her mind. I think.

"Well, neither do I and that's why I'm going over. I can tell you on Saturday, after I meet them," I reassured her.

"It's not like Australia, Ali. You'll have to trust me."

I told her that I trusted her but when she was asleep that night I sneaked out and visited my new friend, and his family. I knew I loved her. I knew I feared losing her respect and trust. But there was something so powerful inside me yelling, "You're old enough! You can do whatever you want!" While the other little voice inside me – more in the background this time round, rattled on about "You'll be sorry. You always are." It sounded like an echo from some distant place. Looking back, I think I was suffering from momentary insanity.

CHAPTER 9

Not for Tourists

I was a changed person by the time I got home from my adventure in the poorer parts of Cairo with Hany. I had decided on the spur of the moment. No plans. No thoughtful consideration. No idea of possible consequences. I was away from home – Aunty Nelly didn't know where I was – for two whole days. This is how it began.

Hany had also sneaked off from his home and he had not told his parents where he was going. His family had been worried sick. But the Egyptian grapevine being what it is, they found out where he was way before we arrived at his house. Being young and dumb, we didn't grasp the magnitude of what we were doing, and all in all, we didn't care. I had a bit of money in my pocket, and it was late autumn. Escaping through the balcony of our flat a few stories up, meant I had to ditch my jacket. I did, however, manage to keep my cap on. It had become a part of me whenever I went out. Hany and I met at the appointed place at *Rabia al-Adawiya* square and caught a bus 'downtown'. In years to come this beautiful place was destroyed in the revolution to oust President Mubarak.

Now I never did come to know where 'downtown' was exactly. Whenever I asked anyone, they would wave a hand in a certain direction that took up much of east and south. So, the best bet was to catch a bus and just observe. Hany could speak simple English and half the fun of being together was me trying to get him to understand what I was saying and vice versa, which included much gesturing and face making. Me with my pathetic attempts at Arabic and he, with his hilarious attempts at English. Hany had a natural sense of humour, and we usually had the bus load of people laughing - hysterically. Even though we were travelling at night, the streets were busy, and the buses were crowded, and time flew. But when we got off the bus in the back streets of Giza, I became strangely silent. My mood changed.

Twisted and coiled over the crumbling buildings like metallic cobwebs were intricate laces of electrical tubes and wires. We had inadvertently stepped out of our time into a backward place. A place devoid of so many modern conveniences. Things like electricity plugs. People would twist a few wires together and then boil a kettle to make tea or connect a television. These areas were just next to places known for their wealth and luxurious living.

The progress of the modern parts of the city lay in contrast to the fragile, temporary nest of huts and makeshift shelters that might be swept away by a random visit from the local police or a neighbourhood feud. If their fragile electrical system was dismantled, the people could no longer run a fan in the hot summer, keep an antiquated, rusted fridge working or, more importantly, a television broadcasting the latest soccer match.

The permanent buildings were ancient and run-down. Stone facades, once impressive, were crumbling, grimy and patched up haphazardly. Makeshift huts were put together with pieces of wrought iron, wood, tarpaulins, and even sheets of plastic. There were whole areas of these huts, and they could be found in between the derelict buildings. People lived where they could. Bare electrical wires danced in the breeze, hovering dangerously close to where people walked, and children played. Everywhere I looked there were small balconies jutting out into the narrow streets. At times these balconies were so close to the other on the opposite side of the street that if you were to outstretch your hand to give something to your neighbour, you could do so easily.

Most buildings were about three or four storeys high, and the projecting terraces would offer shade on a hot day to those below. Day and night there were people walking along the streets and alleys. Women hovering at windows – their hair covered neatly – held babies and toddlers (rugged up against the cold) on window ledges, so the little ones could see the sights below made visible by light bulbs glowing dimly in the street. A family lived in a small space between the stairwells. They were eating on the floor, huddled over a kerosene stove. They waved to Hany and stared at me.

"You know me, you their friend," Hany assured me.

"*Salam alaikum Hagga* Ramadan," Hany greeted the man of the house. *Hagga* Ramadan, smiled between mouthfuls of his dinner and waved us over to join them, but Hany put his hand up and told him politely that we were in a hurry to get to his uncle's house. We were waved on and promised to visit on our return trip.

As we walked along the narrow-crowded streets, I basked in my newfound freedom. I felt like an adventurer, an explorer, a pioneer. I sensed the shift in culture and was curious to discover more. My mind was racing with the images of poverty and deprivation. But I also could not get over the warmth and kindness of the people towards us and towards each other. Then I noticed something that made me stop in my tracks. Hany looked at me and then at the shop. It was a tiny space, just large enough for an ironing board and a bench, where pristine, well-ironed clothes were carefully placed.

"What's wrong?" asked Hany. He too had stopped and was waiting for me to move.

He looked confused. It was, after all, an ironing shop. There are many throughout Cairo. I stopped and stared as the ironing man picked up a glass of water on the side of the ironing board, took a mouthful of water, swished it around his mouth, then proceeded to squirt it from his mouth onto the clothing he was ironing. The iron sizzled and steam rose from the dampness. Didn't he know about plastic spray bottles? The thing is, he did it with such precision! He had obviously been trained and had practiced this procedure until he was an expert.

I remembered how Aunty had sent my clothes to be ironed. My hands inadvertently felt my shirt and trousers. Had they been ceremoniously spat on too? I wanted to shriek and run wildly. But most of all I wanted to throw up. And I did. All over the entrance to the shop. Without asking why, Hany hurried me away while the ironing man and passersby shook their heads and carried on.

Despite the squalid conditions, the people were not miserable. Faces might be serious at first glance, but if eye contact was made, a ready smile was available.

People seemed to know each other and absolutely

everyone knew Hany.

"Don't worry Ali. You are with me. Don't worry."

"Should I be worried?" Why did he keep saying that? I had felt safe from the time I'd arrived in Egypt. Perhaps he was speaking to my unusual silence, the wrinkles on my brow, the absence of a smile from my face. Apart from the unusual methods of ironing clothes, things were quite normal. Crowded. A bit smelly. Lots of flies. But one thing was different.

"These people are so poor," was all I could think. They weren't poor like they didn't have the latest phone or fashionable clothes. Most people wore old, roughly mended clothes, and wore worn- out shoes or sandals, or they walked bare foot. I felt awkward. Guilty. I was here by choice. It was an adventure, and I could remove myself any time I liked. To them, it was their life.

Sensing my discomfort, Hany linked his arm in mine, and we trotted through the dusty streets, heading for his uncle's house.

As we weaved our way deeper and deeper into the labyrinth, (I could no longer recognize our direction and if Hany left my side, I would have no idea where to go) the streets became narrower and narrower until there were no more cars, carts or even motorbikes. Just the odd bicycle swerved out of our way, and we had to stand flat, pressed against the building to let it pass. Light bulbs swaying in the breeze in building entrances lit our way and families huddled beneath them in the quietness of the evening.

Children huddled under streetlamps doing their homework. The neighbourhood kids would congregate under the streetlights, books and pencils in hand, to complete their schoolwork. I felt ashamed when I saw them. I vowed that I would never complain again about studying at a desk with a proper lamp, in a comfortable, safe home. I was filled with a mixture of gratitude and guilt.

In one such street I saw an old man frying *ta'amaya*, eggplant and chips. He had a mini kitchen on a small cart that could be moved by hand. It was like a large, flat wheelbarrow. He was the only person I saw on my escapade that didn't smile. Perhaps it was my red hair that caught his eye. Under his gaze I tried to make myself smaller and I unconsciously pushed my long curls under my cap.

"Don't worry," repeated Hany, "that's *Hagga*

Ahmad. He's crazy but no harm. Don't worry."

There, he had said it again. 'Don't worry.' I was becoming paranoid.

Fried Foods Cook continued to stare at me with eyes that seemed to shout. He held me in my place, rooted to the ground, as if he had physically grabbed my shoulders. He was tall and lean and wore a small black cap on his balding head. His shoulders were stooped, and his clothes were ragged but clean. He wore sandals on his calloused feet.

"Why is he looking at me like that?" I asked, fixed to my spot, watching the old man.

"Before. Long time ago, he was in a war. Now when he sees a foreigner, he gets angry," stated Hany.

I started to think. Did my grandparents fight in a war? Hang on, yes, my mother's grandfather's relative somewhere up the family tree had fought in Gallipoli, I think. I don't know if any of my ancestors had fought against Egypt. Maybe I reminded him of someone?

"Come on," said Hany amiably, "we're nearly there."

I started to move forward, but I couldn't help staring at the old man whose eyes looked at me as if he

knew who I really was. I stopped again and stared at
Hagga Ahmad. I didn't want to be rude or to offend him.
I felt drawn to him. He was poor, no doubt about it. His
mini kitchen was neat and clean but obviously old and
well-used. Small, brightly coloured enamel plates were
stacked in the corner. There was a bucket of soapy water
hitched to the side of the cart to wash them in after the
customer had eaten. His brown face was encased with
deep lines. His mouth downturned in a permanent frown.

"Does *Hagga* Ahmad have a family?" I asked
quietly.

"No. All dead."

"Is this his job? Cooking food?"

"*Hagga* Ahmad was doctor but when he go crazy,
no more doctor."

I nodded. I could see the point. I could not imagine
Hagga Ahmed dressing a wound, prescribing medicine,
or looking at someone's sore throat. No family, no more
career. Maybe that is why he is so sad – and angry, and a
bit crazy. I was sorry. I wanted to go up to him and say,
"I'm sorry *Hagga* Ahmad. I'm sorry you have to live
here and that you don't like it. I'm sorry that you are
alone. I'm sorry that I am intruding on your life and

reminding you of sad things."

For that split second, I really meant what I was thinking, and I think *Hagga* Ahmad could tell because his face relaxed a little. That little voice inside me that fought so hard to be heard was chilling out somewhere deep within my psyche, smiling proudly. I was showing empathy. It felt strange, kind of daunting and kind of nice.

Hany had stopped. He walked back to me where I was standing a few metres away from *Hagga* Ahmad, as we stared at each other. There were tears in my eyes. Oh, how embarrassing. I couldn't control them. If I tried to wipe them away everyone would see. So, I blinked about ten times. That helped. *Hagga* Ahmad's face had softened a little. He looked at my face, put his head down for a second or two, then nodded. I moved on. What on earth had just happened?

By the time we reached Hany's uncle's flat it was late, and we only had time to wash quickly, pray and stretch out on the floor, which was already partially covered – like a crisscross tapestry – with sleeping children.

I sunk into a deep, quiet sleep. What seemed like a short time later, I was blasted out of my slumber by the call to prayer early in the morning – *Fajr* prayer. The loudspeakers from the nearby *masjid* were directly in front of the building. I sat upright and shook my head.

For a moment, I wondered where I was. I looked carefully through the fading darkness and saw a huddle of children whispering and giggling behind their hands, looking at me. I knew my hair must look a fright, so taking advantage of the moment I let out a soft growling noise and started to move towards them like a lion shaking its mane. It worked. They screamed and ran into the other room – off limits to us – it was the ladies' section of the house; the doorway covered by a thick curtain.

Hany's family knew that he had left his home and gone out without permission but there did not seem to be any recriminations. Whatever was said, was said quietly and out of earshot.

Coming back from the bathroom, I saw a tall, slender man dressed in a long creamy-coloured *thowb*. He quietly put on a small, white, lacey cap and called Hany to hurry up. I followed in silence. Once outside, 'Uncle' Shaban shook my hand, hugged me, patted my face, and said, "Welcome to Egypt Ali."

Older people are called 'uncle' or 'aunty' out of respect even if they are not related. I liked it. The older people treated me with gentleness and kindness and then it was my turn to show respect.

I smiled at Uncle Shaban, but my tongue could find no words. So, I smiled again. I must have looked like an idiot.

"Hany," I said quietly, running to catch up with him in the growing light of morning. "Your uncle speaks good English."

"Yes, he owns a perfume shop near the Pyramids. His customers are tourists. That's why he speaks English good."

I felt proud that I knew – and was accepted by – someone who owned a perfume shop near the Pyramids in Egypt. Wow! That is something to tell my Australian mates.

We approached the *masjid* – a small brown, dusty building with dusty carpets covering the dusty floor. When I entered the *masjid,* the men approached me, and we were introduced. I sneezed. Then sneezed again. It was the dust. I was hugged and squeezed and received pats on the back. My body felt broken and bruised from the firm, strong hugs. Were these people made of muscle? But I had never felt so valued and accepted.

"What are we doing today," I asked curiously.

"We eat, go to Pyramids and then a surprise."

"Cool," I thought. I had no idea!

※

We prayed. We walked. Then we walked some more. Poor people don't ride buses unless it's a fair distance. It is all about saving money. I thought I was fit. My feet were aching. I started to hate my life. When would we get there? Hany must have sensed how I felt. He started running.

"What?" I said half to myself.

I staggered after him, limping and pulling faces as the pain in my feet gripped me.

He jumped onto the back of a donkey cart, hitching a ride with another '*Hagga*' who was carting red onions to market. I sat gratefully on top of the onions, resting my poor, tired feet. I looked at Hany and smiled. He started to laugh.

"You smell bad, Ali."

I couldn't let the opportunity pass, so I picked up an onion and pretended to use it as a deodorant, smiling like I was doing a commercial. Hany roared with laughter and the donkey stopped and looked at us. *Hagga* had to whistle and threaten the donkey to make it start trotting again. Hany and I lay down on the pile of onions. We felt like kings.

"Where are we going?" I asked.

"To the Pyramids. Nearly there."

"Oh boy," I said aloud. Again, I had no idea.

CHAPTER 10

It's Just a Camel

It is not an exaggeration to say that I was excited. In fact, I was so enthused that my brain switched off and I entered my inner scattered space where creativity reigns and there are no consequences in sight! We ended up riding camels around the Pyramids that day. Tourists were everywhere. Smiling, spending their money and being curious and excited about everything they saw.

I heard so many languages, my head felt dizzy. I needed some action. I wanted to get into the thrill of things. These were, after all, one of the wonders of the world. I wanted to be a wonder too. That little voice in the back of my mind, said, "Oh no! Not again!"

I approached the camel with gusto. Hany told me to stay calm and not excite the huge beast.

"This guy is calm," I announced, as I acted like a reporter reading the news. "It's just been commandeered by special forces in pursuit of would-be internationally renowned troublemakers."

People actually stopped and watched me. I saw some people looking for the camera I was pretending to talk to. I was rattling off this made-up story and embellishing it with characters, painting a glorious picture of espionage in Egypt. Then I jumped on the camel, waved to the 'camera' and kicked the camel to move. Mistake. Its keeper jumped up, waving a colourful stick telling it in frantic Arabic to do something. He started shouting at the camel and making all sorts of guttural noises. I had jumped onto its back, grasping hold of the pommel on the saddle. Just as well because it lunged forward, got up on its feet and started to run.

"Hang on!" I thought, "That wasn't in my plan!"

As we raced across the desert towards the largest of the Pyramids, my red curls were flying behind me. I was crouched over, holding the saddle for dear life, and trying to look brave. Strangely, those dressage lessons came in handy. I actually kept my heels down, straightened my back and maintained balance. Amazing! Thank you General Ghuraab!

Camel Keeper had mounted another camel and was racing after me, trying to grab my camel's reins. I could see he was angry, and I hoped my camel was faster. My camel just snorted and took off like the Road Runner, leaving them all way behind. I don't remember much after that. But I do remember that it stopped. Like stopped - just like that. Like it put its brakes on and sent sand and dust swirling into the air. Of course, I went flying too. Flying high and far. It felt nice till I hit the ground. Crunch. That was my body hitting rocks. Aunty always said I had a head like a brick. Thankfully she was right, because that day I groaned, stretched, got up, dusted myself off and looked up. I had landed right outside the biggest Pyramid.

"Wow! A Pyramid! A real pyramid," I said. Then I

collapsed and fell to the ground.

Hany came racing up on a horse.

"Get up Ali! We have to leave! Now. My father and uncle heard what happened. Quick."

News travels fast in this place. So, we escaped. If I had wanted an adventure, I got one! It felt like I was in a scene from a movie. I never did get to see inside the Pyramid. Hany found us another donkey cart and we took off like characters from *Heist*. As we rattled off down the road, I heard the frantic clip clop of the donkey's hoofs. We could not find a getaway car! No matter. I wondered if some big movie producer just happened to be there that day. Even though it was a donkey cart escape, I still felt like a star!

Hany's father had to pay Camel Owner money.

Camel Owner had accused me of trying to steal his camel and escaping with it! And then he mentioned something about spies in Egypt! He even threatened to call the police. Why would I do such a thing – on purpose? I'm not a thief. Just having a bit of fun. That little voice inside me cried out, "Get real! It's time to get serious!" I did not listen. I was too busy thinking about what surprise Hany had in store for me.

※

Hany and I finally reached the place he had been telling me about. He promised me swimming. Fun. I was ready. I was still pumped up from the camel jockey experience and the donkey cart escape and I was managing to ignore the growing aches that were creeping all over my body.

We finally arrived at the 'swimming place' as Hany called it. He was so excited and happy to be sharing this with me that I couldn't help but smile. I looked at it. Was it a creek? It looked like a creek. It was too small for a river. Was it a canal? Yeah, maybe a canal. Later I discovered it was one of the many canals in the area where people throw away their rubbish, dead animals or whatever they don't want in their houses or on the streets. It was basically an open sewer. And in I went!

Hany took off his shoes and shirt, smiled warmly to me and jumped in. "Come on," he beckoned.

I froze. I think I still had an idiotic smile on my face. It communicated confusion, disbelief. I gulped. It didn't look very inviting, but I knew I had to dive in too or Hany would never be my friend again. He would be insulted. I had to choose between probable parasites and long-term disease, or friendship. I chose friendship.

I remember saying *Bismillah* as I dived in. Then it all became a blur. There was only one solid object in that part of the canal, and I dove right onto it. It was easily concealed beneath the murky, sludgy water. I whacked my head and went out cold. Apparently, I was dragged out of the canal and somehow taken back to Hany's house. His uncle had forgiven me for the camel escapade when he saw my poor face, my bleeding head, and the rest of 'poor me'. My hair was a tangle of whatever it carried out of the canal. Indescribable bits and pieces of refuse. My face was scratched and grazed, my head had a massive, painful bump, and my arm had a deep cut on it. Bacteria were fighting each other for access – to me. I had become a haven for bacteria.

A doctor came to the house and stitched me up on the spot. Gave me three different injections, patted me on the head and laughed as he went out the door. I felt sore and tired and embarrassed, and I was starving hungry.

"Don't worry Ali. Food is nearly ready."

I felt like I hadn't eaten in days. I was so hungry I was even thinking about the red onions on the donkey cart and licking my lips.

"I wonder what's for lunch?" I thought.

As it turned out we were brought a huge bowl of boiled eggs, bread, and pickles. I looked at the food like it was from a five-star restaurant and tucked in. Between us, Hany and I ended up eating two dozen eggs and I don't know how much bread. The pickles were delicious! We finally lay down and fell fast asleep.

Later that night, I stirred in my sleep. I caught a vibe. I heard a familiar sound. The echo of tiny heels and Arabic being spoken with a definite Scottish twang. "Oh no," I thought, "this is the end. Aunty has found me."

I was whisked out of the house, half carried along empty streets and more or less tossed into a waiting car. I had blurry thoughts of espionage stories. The stories I had told while on the camel somehow became real to my concussed brain. Was it true? Was I being kidnapped? I fell unconscious. Again.

"So, you've had yourself a wee adventure Laddie?" asked Aunty when I came round. I attempted to look at her, but my eyes felt strangely tired and swollen. I couldn't reply except to say, "*Sowwy* (sorry) Aunty. I know I'm a *foow* (fool)."

"At least you're honest," was her only reply.

My little voice inside me, nodded. Exasperated and silent. It turned its back on me.

Aunty didn't talk much. I was waiting for a lecture. After a while I was hoping for one. Finally, I almost begged. Why wasn't she talking to me? I couldn't read her face. She didn't look at me. The lights were dim, and I was put to bed. Next morning, she marched into my room, whisked open the curtains and looked at me. She nearly fell over.

"Ach Laddie! What's happened to ye? Ye look like a plucked chicken!" She covered her face with her hands and collapsed on the floor laughing.

"*Pwucked* (plucked) *nicken* (chicken)?" I said out loud. "Aunty that's *widicuwous* (ridiculous!)." I couldn't speak properly! My tongue was swollen, and somehow connected to the roof of my mouth. My lips seemed disconnected from my body.

"Noo (not) nii (nice) to aaay (say) to yoow (your) *favouwit* (favourite) nephewww (nephew)."

I stumbled out of bed, my eyes barely opening. They just wouldn't do what I was telling them to do! I squinted into the full-length mirror in my room. I was wearing shorts and a singlet top. I saw - without any doubt – that some strange alien being had taken over me.

My red curls were matted and sticking up in all directions. My face was bruised and swollen and puffy, the bump on my head made it look grossly out of shape, and the whole of my body was covered in tiny red, puckered spots. I looked like a chicken that had just been plucked. "Aunty, *yoow* (you're) *'wight* (right)! I *wook* (look) *wike* (like) a *pwucked* (plucked) *nicken* (chicken)!"

My lips were so swollen I slurred every word. I repeated, 'I *weewy* (really) *oo* (do) *wook wike a pwucked nicken*'."

I could not believe what I was seeing. Had I died and gone to Hell? Then Aunty Nelly woke me from my self-induced trance.

I was in a daze. But I heard clearly enough. Sounds of laughter filled the air. I thought Aunty might die from laughter.

"It's *snot wunny* (not funny)," I added.

She paid no heed.

She took photos of me then told me to lie down. The doctor came. His eyes wide in horror when he saw me.

"He doesn't always look like this, right? Do you

have a photo of how he usually looks?"

Aunty brought one.

"Hmm," was all he said.

He was actually stifling a giggle.

"What's *wong* (wrong) *wif* (with) you *peopw* (people)?" I tried to say.

"Young man, is it true you swam in a canal downtown?" he asked.

"*Yeth* (yes), and *wode* (rode) a camel and in a donkey *'art* (cart) and there *wew* (were) onions. And we ate eggth (eggs). *Wots* (lots) and *wots* (lots) of eggth (eggs)," I slurred.

"How many eggs?" he asked. "Two?'"

I shook my tired head.

"Six?"

I closed my swollen eyes.

"Ten?"

I pulled a face and looked away.

"A dozen!?"

I shrugged my shoulders.

"Okay," was all he said.

He proceeded to give me three injections and two big spoons of a brown liquid that burned my throat. I collapsed back onto the bed gasping. Aunty had settled down by now and was sitting politely at my bed side. The doctor explained my treatment and left.

I felt sorry for myself. My body was yelling at me but not with words, with aches and spasms. I knew what it meant to say. I had messed up – again. This time, it could have cost me my life. When I heard the story related back to me about my now-famous dive into the canal, I realize I could have ended up in a wheelchair or even worse – dead. I was like a dog licking its wounds and cowering in a corner. Only I wasn't afraid of being mistreated by anyone but myself. Aunty looked at me and she knew. She knew I regretted what I'd done. But I had to tell her that I was sorry.

I grabbed her hand as she sat next to me. She was deep in thought. In a gesture that would have put any knight in the age of chivalry to shame, I said, "I'm *tho* (so) *thorry* (sorry)."

"What for exactly?" she inquired, with a raised eyebrow.

I think she just wanted to hear me embarrass myself with my slur.

"For *wunning* (running) away."

She patted me on the hand.

"I was waiting for you to do something like that. It took you long enough. Why didn't you do it before?" She was genuinely curious. There was not a judgemental bone in her tiny body. I really didn't know how to answer her. I felt strangely wrong. Should I have boldly run away before? There seemed no end to the expectations people put on me.

"*Whaa* (what)?" Was all I could say.

"I know I've been pushing you, Laddie. But you really have done so well. So remarkably well. It was only when ye hadn't come home by the second night, that I felt I had to tell yer father.

I had half hoped that my pitiful sight would prevent any consequences of my escapades. No such luck.

"You do know Laddie that I had to call your father when you didn't come home," she repeated. She looked sorry.

I sat upright. I didn't register the pain anymore. I hadn't thought of that. Dad? Coming here? To take me home? I didn't want to go, did I?

"He is on a plane right now." She said these words

quietly. Regrettably.

"One phone call, my boy would have saved a lot of trouble."

She was right. I hadn't thought of that.

CHAPTER 11

D-Day

Yes, D-day. D for dad. And doom. And disaster. He arrived with a grey cloud hovering over his balding head. If he ever loved me, he didn't show it then. All I saw in his face was disappointment and anger. Surely, he knew about my academic successes and increasing basketball and dressage abilities. He already knew about my usual charm and confidence. But all he wanted to focus on was the 'canal day'. I must say my emotions were up too.

I had grown taller, and fuller. Well, as full as a skinny red-headed kid can be. But I felt grown-up and misjudged and I was ready to fight. Fight for what, you ask. Fight for my, umm, dignity? Accomplishment? Changes?

I didn't have to as it turned out.

The day after his arrival, dad sat in the living room. Not even jet lag could come near him. He sat composed and silent. Like a brick wall. I remembered the Berlin Wall Aunty had taught me about. Yes, the Berlin Wall. Untouchable. And yet it had been broken down. Aunty broke down his 'Berlin Wall' that day! I didn't know where to look or what to say. I expected a tirade from him, but I got silence. And I didn't know what to do with that.

I could hear him and Aunty talking in quiet, intense whispers from the adjoining room. Did they honestly think I couldn't hear them? Well, I could hear some of what they said. It was about me. Voices went from harsh whispers to blatant shouts! Words darted from one end of the room to the other and bounced off walls and under doors and hurt my ears and my heart.

'Loser'. 'Good for nothing'. 'A waste of money'.

Those were dad's words.

Then I heard: 'Intelligent', 'funny', 'adventurous', 'resourceful'. I love you Aunty!

I decided to walk into the room. They were talking about me after all, and I was – dare I say – nearly grown-up.

Aunty had squared off on dad and was standing on tippy toes with her neck craned so she could look at his face as she told him off. I wanted to suggest she stand on a chair, but she had that SMS aimed on dad. It wasn't the time. Dad became strangely silent.

I sat down and listened and watched and learned. I learned how to be purposefully negative – from Dad. And I learned about love, passion, and advocacy from the best of the best!

"He'll leave this place over my dead body!" said Aunty Nelly through clenched teeth.

I had never seen her so agitated – not even at me.

"You want him? After all he has put you through?" asked my father.

I looked at Aunty. Should I be worried? Why did dad have to remind her?

"That boy is a treasure. He doesn't know it yet

because you have never told him, and he won't believe me. He needs to hear it from you. He needs to know he is important and loved – by – you!" She punctuated her words like a pro.

"Go Aunty!" I thought.

I sat back more comfortably in my chair. I looked at dad.

"Some children are a blessing and others are a, a, a curse."

Aunty inhaled sharply.

"How dare you call Ali that!"

There was not a Scottish rrr in sight. Had she lost her accent? As she spoke, she took a step towards him and with every word, he backed up.

"If you want to keep him here, you're welcome. What will become of him? Being home schooled. No real education. He gets into trouble all the time. It's a waste of effort and I wash my hands of him."

And then he said it.

"There's something wrong with that boy!"

I couldn't help it. I stood up and cried out, concentrating to get my words out despite my slurry tongue. "Hey now, take it eathy (easy). There ith (is)

definitewy (definitely) thomething (something) w'ong
(wrong) with aww (all) of uth (us)!"

It didn't come out like I had hoped. It didn't sound
quite right but I hoped he would understand. Neither of
them moved when I spoke, except their heads. They both
turned and looked at me. Aunty tried her best to hide a
smile. Dad looked confused, for just a second.

Aunty practically pushed him out of the room
without even lifting her finger. She just took steps
towards him and steered him with her courage. Soon, he
was gone. I sat for a while then finally heard a suitcase
being pushed and pulled and the front door banged
loudly. I had never felt so loved.

CHAPTER 12

Choices

It wasn't that I didn't want to see my dad. I didn't want to hear what I thought he was going to say. I didn't want the putdowns and insults and labels. But I did see him the next day. Aunty had thoroughly shamed him. He approached me with a mixture of shame and blame but he gave me a rushed hug, and said, "You can stay if you want. I'll send money."

I nodded. Money is good. There were so many thoughts crashing into each other in my head that I couldn't find the words to express them. The little voice deep down inside of me was shouting, "Just be nice! Say thank you." I listened.

It was strange how my dad reacted when I said, 'Thanks Dad'. He looked at me, waiting for a sarcastic comment. But it never came. I smiled. I reached out and shook his hand and promised to email him. Zoom would be way too awkward. Then he was gone.

There was one thing that Aunty was wrong about. She had told Dad that I didn't believe her when she told me I was a – what was it? – 'a treasure'! But I did believe her. In fact, I carried her warmth and love and confidence in me wherever I went. I still have it today.

Of course, I decided to stay in Egypt and live my life surrounded by noise, dust, and chaos. I just wanted to be with my Aunty Nelly. Afterall, she loves me spots and all. Now, to me, that is real love. I dare anyone to beat that!

CHAPTER 13

More Changes

After my dad left and I continued living with Aunty Nelly in Egypt, my future seemed a little uncertain. Not bleak. Just not mapped out. Before there was this timeline. We had a routine. I knew what was coming. It made me feel safe. The one-year timeline had disappeared along with my dad. What had started out as one year in Egypt, now flowed out into my future with no end in sight. Maybe I shouldn't have been worried, but I like to know what's happening. Life is so unpredictable. When things are uncertain, that scattered, risk-taking part of me raises its adventurous head and trouble follows. Aunty knew that about me. Again, she had the answer.

※

"Don't go thinking ye can slack off now Laddie!" she announced early one morning.

"The thought never crossed my mind," I answered. I was laying down on the couch in my pjs and dressing gown with a stripy woollen hat over my hair. Blue and white – Geelong Football Club! Come on the Cats! My feet were encased in fluffy socks. I told myself I was having a 'mental health day'. Life has been stressful.

When Aunty Nelly marched in and made her announcement, I was startled and defensive. Just because I was lounging on the couch watching cartoons and eating chips, didn't mean I was slacking off. I sat up straight but continued munching and crunching my way through the enormous bag. Sour cream and chives. Yum!

"So, you think that's breakfast, do ye?"

Aunty was on the war path. As quietly as I could, without taking my eyes off the cartoons, I pushed the bag of chips behind a cushion.

"Of course not, Aunty. How could anyone eat chips for breakfast! That was, a, um, pre-breakfast snack. What's for brekky?"

I turned and looked at her face on. She was staring down at me.

"Have ye made yer bed?"

She didn't wait for an answer.

"Why aren't ye dressed?"

Had she been taking lessons from the General?

"It's time ye learned to cook. Get up!" The pitch of her voice was rising with every word she spoke. I had to move fast or cover my ears.

I followed her meekly into the kitchen and learned how to organize a healthy, tasty breakfast. I was at home in the kitchen. I could make toast without a second thought. Tea. Coffee. Hot chocolate. No problem. I could even boil eggs if I put my mind to it. But I had never actually had more than two things on the table or my plate at the same time when I was in control of mealtimes. This was totally new.

"From now on you'll be doing this every morning on your own," she announced.

I looked from left to right, averting her gaze.

"Um okay," I said. I was rather proud of myself as we sat down soon after. Sausages, scrambled eggs (that was new!), olives, cheese, bread, and pickles. I still scratched unconsciously whenever I came face to face with a boiled egg. But, you know, life goes on.

"Is there something you want to tell me Aunty?" I ventured.

She wasn't her normal self.

"Aye Laddie." She put her cup of tea down, sat back and stared at me.

"I'm not going to homeschool you anymore Ali."

I stopped chewing and looked at her. No homeschool? That means school! School? With students, teachers and white boards and homework and rules? I panicked.

"Aunty I'm not going to school." I meant it.

"You will start online studies through the Australian Distance Learning curriculum. You will have daily classes, homework, deadlines, and expectations."

She didn't wait for it all to sink in. She continued, "I'll oversee your studies but it's high time you started to take responsibility for yourself. Ye don't need me standing over ye like before. Let's face it Ali, you're a young man now."

I stopped chewing and stared at the wall. I was in shock. Why couldn't things just continue as they were? I had finally got used to the system Aunty and I had going and now everything was going to change. I decided to dig my heels in. That little voice inside, whispered, "Don't bother!"

I got up, pushed my chair aside and stood over Aunty.

"I don't want to! I'm not. You can't make me!" Was I six years old again?

"Sit down Laddie!" she ordered.

I sat. I surprised myself by how quickly I exited 'you can't tell me what to do' mode. Aunty smiled.

"I think you'll like it better Laddie," she said more gently. "You'll make friends online and you can finish VCE and go to an Australian university in the future if you so choose."

I reached for another boiled egg and some pickles and wrapped them in flat bread. I had been put in my place. Again. I munched contentedly and realised that what she said made sense. I did a quick turnaround.

"I see Aunty. It makes sense." I nodded my head.

Why did I cave so easily? The almost-man part of me, rolled his eyes.

"You'll start the first of next month, *Inshallah*," she announced, with her eyes still fixed on me. "I expect excellent results Ali or else..."

"Or else what?" I thought. I didn't dare ask.

"Or else I'll put you in a real school and there will be no basketball because you'll have no time, I assure ye."

I had spoken to my Egyptian mates enough to know that was true. Gruelling daily bus rides, copious amounts of homework and unrealistic expectations. Distance Ed was sounding better all the time.

"Count me in Aunty."

She looked at me confused. I wasn't arguing anymore. I wasn't being sarcastic. Truth is, I really couldn't think of anything to say.

CHAPTER 14

Introducing Noora!

If I was to draw a map of my family tree, it would have swirls and twirls around Britain in mostly coastal regions. We love the sea, us McDougals! It would extend to northern Scotland and the Shetlands and then branch off to Denmark and Norway.

How we landed in Australia is quite another story. It had something to do with grandparents embracing Islam and other family members accepting Islam, or not.

It was all about starting a new life on the other side of the world and then other relatives followed. Many became Muslims and they intermarried, but one thing was a constant. One person in every generation was born with flaming red curly hair. I was the lucky fellow for this generation. I thought I was the only one until Aunty Nelly announced one day that my niece (another long story) also had fiery red locks.

Whenever I think about Noora, I shake my head and cover my face with my hands in exasperation and confusion. You see, I'm her uncle but she is older than me. Yeah, I know! How did that happen? I can hardly wrap my head around it. But I insisted on my 'uncle' status. I only had one niece. And just because she was six months older than me didn't mean she could treat me any old way she liked. You must respect your uncle, right?

Noora is sharp-witted. Aunty Nelly said her tongue should be registered as a lethal weapon. Noora has this shrug she uses whenever she feels like it. Roughly translated, it means 'whatever'. It is infuriating. But my biggest problem with Noora is that Aunty Nelly thinks she is an angel and I'm sure Aunty loves her more than me. I know that sounds childish. But it matters to me, and I hate that it matters.

And Noora is talented. I actually think she has managed to wrap Aunty Nelly around her little finger – something I've been trying to do forever. She was always a rotten little kid and now, I imagine, she is a rotten little teenager. Every year the family comes together for visits, so we have seen each other throughout the years. Aunty just told me she is going to be staying with us. I don't know for how long. I feel like I've been convicted and sentenced to prison with hard labour. I know my life will change. I haven't seen Noora for a while, but I heard from good sources (the family grapevine) that she is a troublemaker. Maybe we share a lot of the same genes. Well, we will see who is better at that! The little voice inside me was saying, "Do you really think Aunty doesn't 'know' her?" That's something to think about.

Anyway, my time with Noora took my life to the next level. Spoiler alert! Tears will be shed.

CHAPTER 15

Rotten Little Kid Grows Up!

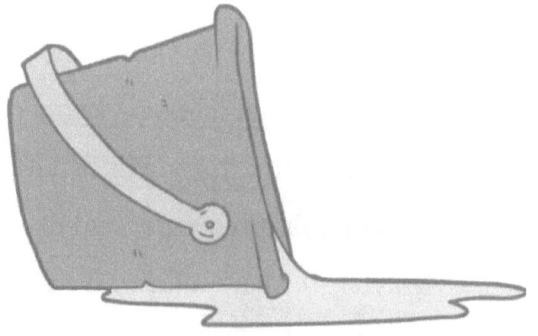

Being the gentleman I am, I went with Aunty to the airport to pick up Noora. I was in no hurry to meet her. My stomach was churning. I felt like I was already defeated. All Aunty had been talking about for days was 'Noora this! And Noora that!' I was sick of Noora even before she arrived. I sat sullen and determined to be negative. Dad would have been proud of me! I tried to stay calm and take it in my stride, but the little voice within me droned on, "You wish."

My eyes scanned the people emerging from the gates. Aunty Nelly stood on tiptoes peering at the crowd of tired travellers. We had almost given up on seeing Noora when someone tapped me on the shoulder. I turned around flustered.

"Your fashion sense has gone downhill, Ali McDougal. You're looking a bit homeless!"

"You!" Was all I could say.

Aunty Nelly grabbed Noora and spun her around in a loving hug. I rolled my eyes and crossed my arms.

Noora winked cheekily at me as she was spun around and around.

"I've missed ye, my bonnie wee lassie!" Big kisses topped it all off. I started to walk away.

The little voice inside me scolded, "Don't be such a baby!"

Was that the moment I decided to be a rebellious teenager again? Whether I liked it or not, I was regressing. Fast. If they thought I was trouble before, they haven't seen anything yet. I was demanding attention! I pulled my cap on backwards, shrugged my shoulders inside my jacket and leaned on one leg, trying to look relaxed and cool. Aunty looked at me and smiled.

She walked up to me, stood on tiptoes – again - and pinched my cheeks.

"Come on Laddie. Carry the bags."

"Yes, 'Uncle' Ali. And you can take this one too!" Noora spoke in a fake little girl voice, trying to be innocent and sweet as she shoved her carry-on into my hands. Life is so unfair!

I ended up with a suitcase and carry-on decorated with little skulls interlaced with purple and pink ribbons.

"That is so you," I thought. "How embarrassing!" I murmured. My eyes scanned the area. No one I knew, thankfully!

I walked slowly just so they would have to wait, but they didn't care. They chatted endlessly and I could feel my anger rising.

Aunty must have noticed I wasn't with them. She turned and called out – so everyone could hear, "Ach Laddie! Step on it now! Do you think I'd let such a smart boy like you get away?"

They giggled. I wanted to punch the air.

"If you're smart, you won't!" I responded casually. I still wanted to punch the air.

※

We were sitting in the living room. I maintained a stony silence. They chatted away. The sound was irritating. Annoying. Unbearable. I decided to study algebra. It would be way more comforting and entertaining than listening to Noora make Aunty laugh and hogging all her attention.

I was just about to get up and leave the room when Noora stood up, faced me, and asked straight up, "Why don't you like me, Ali?"

Her tone of voice was menacing. Sarcastic. Challenging. I took the bait.

"I haven't forgotten the sugar bowl incident," I said without thinking.

The little voice inside me said, "What? What does that have to do with anything?" I ignored it.

Aunty sat back and gave us space. She was listening intently and didn't interrupt.

In just a short time I managed to vent out all the thoughts and feelings I'd been lugging around for ages. And she copped it in one go!

"You're a spoilt little brat! You always think you

can get whatever you want!"

We were face to face. She was as tall as me, but her hair was longer and way curlier. She wore it in beaded braids. I continued.

"You resented me being born your uncle and you've always had it in for me!" I didn't even come up for breath. "You knew that my mum had told me not to put any more sugar in my oatmeal and when she wasn't looking, you poured in a mound of it! I didn't have time to take it off and mum saw me and yelled. She never yells! But she yelled at me and it's your fault!"

I was pointing a bony finger at her, punctuating each word.

"I wasn't allowed to go to the birthday party, and I missed out on Paint Balling. You're right. I don't like you."

I was hissing like a snake. Little specs of spit were flying around our faces. I even scared myself. My little voice inside me said, "Who are you?"

Noora stood straight and put her head a little to one side and said calmly, "We were five years old. You have quite the memory."

That was true. It was about ten years ago. She

hadn't exactly ruined my life. My contorted brain was replaying to me what I had just said. It sounded lame. Had I really been holding onto that for years? My face was glowing red. I knew she noticed.

"If that's the best you can do then I think you're rather pathetic, Ali McDougal."

She was spot on. There was this silence between us. Like a solid wall. I didn't know what to say and that worried me. I always know what to say!

"If you had of said, 'Oh Noora you're so much better looking than me or you're so much smarter or cooler to nicer or friendlier or more amazing, then I would understand. Sugar in oatmeal, pffff."

"Whatever!" she said with a shrug of her shoulders.

I was struggling.

"It's the injustice of it all. You manipulated me."

"Okay, then that makes me smarter."

"But not nicer."

Aunty's head moved as she looked at each of us in turn as we spoke. It looked like she was watching a tennis match.

"Good point," Aunty interjected.

I nodded and smiled. One point for me! Neither of

us responded. We continued to stare each other down. I grew more and more tense with each passing moment.

"You are never ever nice to me," I wailed. I did sound like a baby, but I continued.

"I tried to make you like me, but you just got me into trouble. The 'sugar bowl and oatmeal' incident is only one example."

I wanted to leave the room, leave them both, but my feet wouldn't budge.

"You were always little goody two shoes!" she mimicked sarcastically. "I was forever hearing, 'Why can't you be like Ali? Why can't you be good at school like Ali? Ali! Ali! Ali! I was sick of hearing your name Ali McDougal!"

She drew out the last words, emphasizing, well, me. I scratched my head uncomfortably. Was Noora jealous of me? That was new.

"Your mum and dad got you everything you wanted. You always had heaps of pocket money and you never shared!" I added. I was yelling by now.

"At least you have a mum and dad!" she snapped. And stopped.

"Huh?" I thought. My little voice inside me said,

"Go easy now. Slow down." I did.

"What do you mean? So do you," I retorted.

"My dad just up and disappeared." She spread out the syllables of that last word and moved her hands as she spoke, sweeping them over the top of her head. "He's remarried now and never contacts me. And mum spent so long being sad all the time and ignoring me, then she found someone else and was all happy again and is still ignoring me. I'm just in the way. She sent me to Aunty Nelly. But don't worry Ali. I won't be here long, and you can have Aunty back. I know she dotes on you!"

Tears flooded her face, but her voice was steady. I was gobsmacked. Should I feel guilty? I think so. I wasn't sure. What had I done? Nothing, I think. I didn't know about her parents breaking up and what had happened. All I was thinking about was the 'sugar bowl and oatmeal' incident. I started to feel stupid and childish and insensitive and stupid and childish and....

Aunty got up and gently took Noora by the arm and led her out of the room. I was left standing there feeling like a fool. This would take ages to process. The little voice inside me rolled up its sleeves.

※

Aunty returned to the living room after a while. She sat, yawned, and stretched out, looking right at me. I had been sitting in the darkening room. Night had enveloped it. I hadn't bothered to switch on a light. There was something comforting in the darkness.

"Ach Laddie! Do ye feel better now that ye got all that out of yer system?" Aunty did not look pleased.

"Actually, I don't. I don't feel better. I feel rotten."

Aunty Nelly stifled another yawn.

"Why didn't you tell me about Noora's parents getting divorced and why she came here?" I asked seriously.

"Ye never bothered to ask me. Ye only thought about the past and yourself."

That was true. I could have asked. Aunty would have told me. "But if you'd told me, I would have handled things differently." I wanted to cast blame on Aunty. Not on myself.

"Ye didn't 'handle' anything Ali. You reacted to your own emotions. Handling requires rational thinking. There wasn't any of that."

Oh no! She was right again. I sat in grim silence.

The 'uncle' part of me wanted to make things better. The almost-man part of me agreed wholeheartedly. The little voice inside me was nodding its head furiously. But I had no idea how to rectify the situation. I was at a loss.

"I don't know what happened Aunty."

I looked sad and lost.

"Listen Laddie. Relationships are like an eclipse. You think they've gone but they're just hiding. They'll come out again. You two were always close."

We were?

"But what hides the relationship Aunty? What stops us from seeing it for what it is?"

"Ohh things like ego, selfishness, not being switched on."

It felt like an eclipse. Everything felt dark, including me.

Again, Aunty knew exactly what to say.

"Laddie. Just be nice to Noora. Be there for her. Meet her halfway. Show her the ropes. She isn't acquainted with Egypt like ye are."

That sounded easy enough. I could do that. I could make Noora feel like she had someone looking out for her. I was hopeful. I had no idea.

CHAPTER 16

Going for a Little Drive

For the most part, Aunty Nelly is easy going, especially when it comes to her belongings. But one thing that is sacred and out-of-bounds is her car. She has been driving for years in Cairo traffic and despite all the chaos and traffic congestion, she has never had an accident. Not even a scratch or a dent!

One time! Just one time I started up her car and reversed it up the driveway. I thought she was going to call the police! But I'm quick to learn. I never even looked like I wanted to drive it again. Noora, however, had a lot to learn.

I had prepared breakfast for everyone. It was my job after all. Noora bounced into the room, glanced at the set table, and shook her head.

"I'm not eating that stuff!"

"How rude!" I thought.

I got up from the table and walked over to her.

"Gratitude! Gratitude Noora! Look it up. It's a thing," I declared.

"Can I ask you something Ali?" She was speaking more sweetly now.

"Can I stop you?"

"Hmm. Nope!" she said. "I want you to take me out today. I feel like some adventure."

"That doesn't sound good at all," I thought. Then I remembered my promise to Aunty; that I would stay beside her and show her the ropes.

"Uh okay. What do you have in mind?" I asked.

Without a word, she snatched up her backpack,

grabbed Aunty's car keys from the hook in the hallway and headed out the door.

"What the….?" I said aloud. I slipped on my shoes, grabbed some food from the table and followed her.

Aunty was still asleep. She hadn't been feeling well. That's why Noora had the opportunity to make a break for it. I did some quick thinking. Going with her was the right thing to do? I wasn't convinced. I followed her into the street where Aunty's car was neatly parked in front of the building.

"Noora!" I called. "You know you are not allowed to drive! I mean you can't drive. You don't have a licence, and this is Aunty's car, and she doesn't let anyone touch it, let alone drive it. Let's go back inside." I was desperate. I knew it was hopeless.

"Ohh it's a scary day for Ali today." She was mocking me. "Will Aunty Nelly be upset with you for not 'looking after me'?" She was talking in that annoying little girly voice. I scowled.

"Too right she will," I thought. I mean, I wanted to be the uncle and all that but not with all the responsibility that goes with it. Life is tough!

"I'm not afraid," I said in a cool, calm, and collected voice. Who was I kidding?

She started to unlock the car door. I lunged at her and grabbed the keys and held them high in the air. She jumped up as high as she could, but my arms are long. They actually grew first and the rest of me is catching up! She grabbed at me, but she knew it wouldn't work. She stopped and confronted me.

"You know I'm going to drive today whether you like it or not Ali McDougal!"

"Oh yeah?" I showed her the keys then chucked them into the street where cars and other vehicles were rushing along.

"No! Ali! Why did you do that?" She pushed me against the car and took off towards the road.

She was about to weave her way into the traffic to look for the keys but I grabbed her just in time as a taxi came whizzing past.

"Are you crazy?" I asked.

"A bit, I think." She stood on the pavement, looking sad.

I was relieved that she was no longer threatening me with the busy street. I heaved a sigh of relief.

The first of many that day.

"I'm a bit cold Ali. Can I wear your jacket."

She looked gloomy and pathetic. Little did I know, I was being conned.

Without a thought, I took off my jacket and gave it to her. She put it on, reached into the pocket where I had hidden the keys before I pretended to throw them, and unlocked the car door.

"I saw you put them in your pocket Ali. Do you think I'm an idiot?"

I was flabbergasted. She didn't miss a thing. There was nothing else to do but jump in the front passenger seat and pray.

CHAPTER 17

Another One Bites the Dust

I kept myself as low in my seat as I could. I didn't want anyone I knew to see me. Noora had a brightly coloured bandana woven around her beaded locks. I wasn't sure which was brighter, the bandana or her red hair. She looked like a neon sign, drawing attention to me!

Her face was fully focused on the road, and I had to

admit she was a good driver. But I didn't want to ask her where she had learned to drive. I really didn't want to talk to her at all. She had put me in a dilemma, and I couldn't help but worry what would happen when Aunty got up and saw that Noora and I, and her car, were gone. I closed my eyes and shook my head.

"So where do you want to go Ali McDougal?"

"Home." I meant it.

"Forget home. We are on an adventure. I want to go downtown. Do you know the way?"

"Nope."

Even if I knew, I would never tell her.

"Why didn't you just ask Aunty to let you drive her car?"

"Are you kidding? That would give her the opportunity to say no and this way I haven't disobeyed anyone. No one told me not to take the car."

She tried to look innocent.

"I did."

"You don't count! You're my partner in crime now."

That was too true to be funny.

She was weaving in and out of traffic like a pro. No

indicating, just carefully timed manoeuvres that left screeching brakes, honking horns and curses in Arabic behind us. I pulled my cap over my face.

As we cruised along Tehran Street and turned into the Autostrade, I noticed the streets were lined with soldiers who had their backs to the road. All neatly lined up, a few metres apart. I also noticed the traffic was much lighter now. Then I looked again and saw we were the only car on the road. Weird. My little voice inside me was strangely silent.

"This is great," observed Noora. "We will get there in no time. No traffic! What did you say before about the streets being crowded. Huh!"

She sped up. Foot to the floor on the accelerator. That's when I noticed our little car was being surrounded by five large black cars with heavily tinted windows.

"What's going on?" I asked, half to myself.

"They'd better move over and let me pass if they know what's good for them," said Noora, her foot to the floor.

The black cars drew closer and squeezed us between them as we roared down the road in the tiny car.

"I think you'd better stop. Noora! Stop!"

She ignored me as usual. Then I looked to my left and saw a gun pointed at us from the back window of the shiny black car! I looked to my right and saw the same thing. I froze but my mouth kept talking.

"Noora! They have guns." Then it dawned on me.

"I know what's happening! This is the president's entourage! We are in the middle of it. Noora!"

"Wow this is cool. Just like the movies!" Then she acted like she was slowing down and when there was a space between the cars, she darted through it and made a sharp left into Yousef Abbas Street. She was driving as fast as she could go.

The entourage closed their windows. Guns disappeared. They continued on their way. But in their wake, they sent a police motorbike that was tailing us. The road was empty except for us in Aunty's car and the big burly policeman on the motor bike. The roar of the bike was loud, and he revved it up and flashed his lights behind us.

"Noora! Stop the car. Let me explain to him."

Explain? Explain what? That my crazy niece had stolen my Aunty's car? That my life would be over when I got home. That I couldn't get Noora to do what I asked.

That she was unreasonable. Hmm. Maybe this was an opportunity to get rid of her once and for all, and hand her over to Big Burly Policeman!

The little voice inside me shouted, "Don't be ridiculous. That's not nice. They'll probably take you too!" I gulped.

I started to speak again but she told me, "Be quiet Ali. I'm concentrating. I'll handle this."

Strangely, I was confident that she would handle it, but I had no idea how.

She revved the motor hard. Sped up and when Big Burly Policeman was directly behind us, inches away, she slammed on the brakes! Big Burly Policeman slammed on his brakes too and went flying. I closed my eyes. I didn't want to see what would happen. I heard the motorbike skid and a loud bang. Noora laughed.

"Gotcha! Ten points for me!" she said out loud.

Ten points? Did she think this was a game?

She turned into a small street. I looked behind us and saw Big Burly Policeman rubbing his back and legs and limping to his bike. He was okay. I closed my eyes and felt a wave of relief. One of many that day.

"That was great!" cried Noora. "What a day!"

"When are you leaving?" I asked her angrily. She had slowed down in the small streets. She looked relaxed.

"It's time you put this visit out of its misery!" I added irritably.

"Oh! Cheer up. The day is just beginning. This will be a blast," she announced cheerfully.

I looked at her sideways. Her concentration level was on par with a goldfish! She had completely forgotten and overlooked the danger that had surrounded us just a short time ago. I must be crazy to be in the car with this person. But Aunty had told me to stay with her. I had no choice.

CHAPTER 18

It's Not Over Yet

I sat sulking in the front seat of the car. I couldn't remember the last time I smiled. I was literally there for the ride. I consoled myself that I had to be with her and show her the ropes. Those were the instructions. I imagined I had to prevent her from being kidnapped. But then who in their right mind would kidnap Noora?

Surely, they would return her quick smart. No amount of money would be worth it! No one, and I mean no one could put up with her for long!

Noora followed the road signs and we found ourselves in *Khan al Khalini* market. This is a tourist hot spot. I had been here before with Aunty. You can get everything a tourist could desire. Cute little stuffed camels. Egyptian-looking artifacts. Clothing – ancient and modern designs. Silver. Leather goods. To name just a few. The narrow laneways were interlaced in intricate maze-like patterns. It was easy to get lost. If you entered a shop, someone would appear and bring you tea in a tiny glass cup and let you sit down. They would make you feel important and valued as they ripped you off! No Egyptian would go shopping in *Khan al Khalini* market unless the haggling reached a crescendo and a fair price was eventually agreed upon. It could take ages. In the process, the customer would walk off several times and be followed and politely invited back to the shop. It was fun to watch.

"You don't have any money Noora. Why do you want to come here?"

"Ali McDougal! You have no imagination. I don't have any money right now. Watch and learn."

She parked the car on a side street. I looked around

feverishly to find landmarks so I could find my way back to it. I was terrified to go home and face Aunty with the car in tow but without it, I dare not think.

I grabbed the keys from her and put them carefully in my pocket. She returned my jacket to me and then proceeded to remove her shoes and socks. She put them and her backpack in the boot of the car. Then she proceeded to tear her shirt front and long sleeves and scrape dirt onto them. She also rubbed dirt on her face and over her bandana and her baggy jeans. She scuffed her feet in the dirt and tried to black out one tooth. Then she faced me, smiling and asked, "How do I look?"

"Like the crazy idiot you are," I remarked. "What are you doing now?"

I had never scratched my head so much in one day.

"Don't you look around you Ali? Can't you see all the beggars? They are raking in the dough! And I want my share. I want some money too."

She waved her finger around the area and pointed out several beggars. Tourists were handing them money. Lots of money. The beggars looked pitiful. Was there some kind of beggar conspiracy going on? I watched as some young boys took their cash to an obese man sitting under a nearby tree. They handed over the money and went back to beg. The man licked his fingers then counted the cash and stashed it inside his shirt. I looked at Noora. She looked pitiful too. Hang on! What?

"Stay here Ali. Don't move. I'll be back."

Before I could say anything, she disappeared into the crowd. I strained my eyes to see where she was. That bandana was hard to miss. She was actually limping and protecting her arm as if it was hurt. Sure enough, when she opened those big green eyes wide and looked sad, tourist after tourist filled her hands with American dollars.

I stared in amazement. "She will get us arrested!" I thought. I had no idea what to do.

After a short time, she returned and pulled my arm, dragging me into a quiet corner.

"I have nothing to do with this!" I whispered through angry clenched teeth. "You're stealing!"

"I am NOT stealing!" She was adamant.

"You're tricking and deceiving well-meaning people. It's just like stealing and I'm having nothing to do with it!" I meant it.

"Honestly Noora! It's like I don't know you.

There's no excuse for doing what you're doing." I felt disgusted with her.

"Aw come on Ali. This is a lot of money. We could have a great day with it, then go home and apologise. Listen to the lecture and then it will all be over."

"Is that what you think?" I asked her. "Unlike you, I really do care about Aunty Nelly. You sound like you're using her. You're disgusting!" I started to walk back to the car. I had the keys now.

I looked back at her. She looked lonely and sad standing under the tree. She wasn't faking that look.

"What's going on with her?" I wondered. Surely, it must be more than just her mum and dad.

Then I saw an Egyptian man on a skateboard moving towards her. He had no legs and was pushing himself along with his hands. His torso rested on the skateboard. As he passed, people nodded to him, smiled, and greeted him. He smiled back. He was obviously friendly and well-liked. His arms were massive, strong. He had the biggest smile on his face. I couldn't believe my eyes. I had never seen anything like this. I wondered what he had to be smiling about. I watched him come next to Noora and hand her some money. Her eyes were fixated on him. She didn't move or say a word. He smiled, made *Duaa* for her, and rolled away. I watched him go. The irony of the situation silenced me. I felt I had been stabbed in the heart. Did Noora feel that too?

It took a while for me to collect myself then I walked up to her ready to tell her off. I was going to tell her it was pure evil that she could take money from that man. That I was ashamed of her. That I wanted nothing to do with her anymore. But when I approached her, I saw she was crying. Not big heaving, loud sobs but silent, choking tears. All the fakeness, daring and bravado had disappeared. Here she stood transparent and vulnerable. It took a man with no legs on a skateboard to touch my niece's heart! But he did. As it turned out, there was no need for the lecture. I think she is starting to learn. The little voice inside me said, "About time."

I took her by the arm and led her over to a bench under a tree. We sat down. I was determined to understand what was going on with her.

"Noora! You can't go on like this. It really is too much." I didn't wait for her to speak. "You are hurting all the people who care about you!"

"Care about me? Me?" she declared in a loud

whisper. "No one cares. No one! You don't! My parents don't! Aunty just feels sorry for me."

"I don't feel sorry for you. I think you're making stupid decisions. Fix it. We can all get along. And you have to give that money away in charity. You have to! It's wrong to keep it!" I was determined. She didn't say no.

The almost-man inside me wanted to smooth things over. Set things on a defined course. But then, life is full of setbacks.

"You don't know what has happened to me. No one knows. No one cares. I'm alone in this world Ali. I have to survive."

"What? You couldn't be alone if you tried. We have this humongous family, and everyone knows everything about everyone else. It's maddening but kind of nice too."

"They don't know all about me. No one does."

"So, tell me. I want to understand. Maybe I can help."

She looked at me closely. Her eyes scanned me like she was looking for an error sign or any indication to build that wall around herself again. I must have passed the test because this time she opened up.

"Ali. It's a sad day in the life of Noora."

So dramatic!

"Something is missing in me. A part that's lost. I don't know how to find it. I can't trust anyone anymore."

What was she talking about?

"Can you get to the point? I don't get it."

She took a deep breath and sighed.

"There is this boy. I liked him a lot and he used to talk to me especially after Dad left and I was feeling really alone. I was sooo angry. I had never felt bad like that, and I didn't know what to do."

Her hands were gesturing nearly every word. If I tied her hands behind her back, she wouldn't be able to communicate!

"This guy, Billy; his real name is Bilal, was nice to me. I trusted him and told him stuff. We used to talk every day. Mum was always in her room on her phone or sleeping or watching TV. I was no longer a part of her life. And Dad was just – well – gone. Not there. He packed his bags and disappeared. So, I did what I wanted."

She stopped talking for a minute. She was

breathing rapidly. I let her calm down. The little voice inside me gave me a hug.

"Anyway, Billy said we should run away together and have an Islamic marriage, but no one needs to know about it. It would be a secret. He told me that everyone does it. Why shouldn't we? I was ready to rebel and do anything to annoy my parents. It all made sense. He was eighteen so I believed he knew lots of stuff I didn't know. Like I say, I trusted him."

I listened silently to Noora. I stared at something on the ground. I could see where this was going, and I didn't like it. The almost-man inside me was shaking his fists.

She continued. "Anyway, after a while he started asking me for photos of myself. He said he wanted to remember me when he was at work. But he kept asking for a different kind of photo." She looked uncomfortable. "Ali, don't make me spell it out! You know what I mean, right?"

I knew. The little voice inside me had its hand over its mouth. I nodded.

"Well, I refused to send him anything like that and then he started to get angry, and he backed off. He never had marriage in his mind and only wanted to use me."

She paused. "You know Ali, he wanted to hurt me in the worst way. And I almost fell for his tricks." She put her thumb and index finger together – almost touching. "This close Ali! Sometimes I can't believe how dumb I am."

"Hang on a second! You didn't though. You didn't fall for his games. You were smart. I'm actually proud of you. You're switched on Noora."

I didn't praise her often. It felt strange. But she looked happy when I spoke. Her face softened. She sighed.

"But I want to ask you Noora. What made you stop and not send the photos?"

She turned and looked at me face on.

"I used to go to classes with girls my age and we had this awesome teacher. She didn't just tell us Islamic stories; you know the usual stuff. She made it real, and she made me want to do the things that all those great people did in the past. She made me want to be like them. Our motto was 'Proud to Be Muslim' and 'Islam 4 Me'. I knew that if I sent those pictures to Billy, I would be really far away from achieving that goal. It would be like sliding down a slippery slope further and further

away from who I want to be. I know I shouldn't have
been talking to him in the first place but sending the
pictures would be way too far. I didn't want to do that."

"Wow," I whispered. "That teacher sounds great."
I was speechless. Wish I had one like that. But hang on, I
have Aunty Nelly. So, we are equal there.

Noora went on. "I think that's when I started to act,
well, a bit different. I got into trouble at school and
generally gave everyone a hard time. I told Mum
eventually. She had a fit. It just made me feel worse. She
made it look like it was all my fault. She never thought
for a second that it had anything to do with Dad walking
out on us or her being sealed off in her room. Billy had
disappeared from my life, and Mum said I should be
grateful to have escaped trouble. But she didn't get it.
She didn't understand that I was so alone and lost. You
know, parents think they can do whatever they want and
us kids will just tag along. But I miss my dad. I used to
think he loved me. I believed it! I was sure! Dam it! Ali!
I'm so angry at him. Why doesn't he want me?"

Tears again. Floods of them. I joined her. I thought
of my own dad and how he was impossible to please.
Impossible to reach. We just sat and cried together. In

later years, Noora told me that this was the moment when she started to heal.

After a little while, she continued. "I was sent here. Mum swore me to secrecy. Something about family reputation." She rolled her eyes. So did I. We wiped our tears and sat in silence. I had wanted to understand and now I did. The almost-man inside me was seething. I wanted to hurt that guy. Bad.

It wasn't long after, that a taxi pulled up beside us and I heard a definite click, click of heels and words being muttered with a whirl of distinct Scottish rrrrrs. We were sprung. Aunty had found us.

The police had recorded her number plate, and she was contacted after the entourage debacle. Thankfully she was able to explain her way out of trouble. I imagined she told them her relative had just escaped from the psych ward and had taken the car without permission. Anyway, whatever she said it worked. But how she found us in *Khan al Khalini* remained a mystery for some time. I began to think Aunty had mysterious connections until one day she told me that she had 'find my car' on her phone. Dah!

CHAPTER 19

Liar! Liar! Pants on Fire!

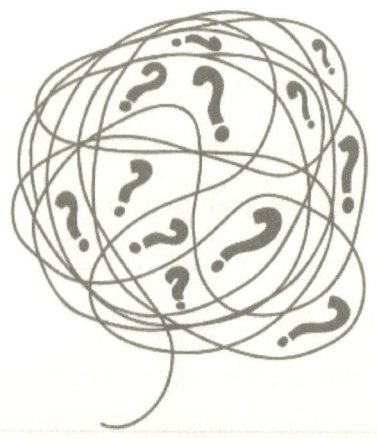

Aunty was strangely silent about Noora and the car fiasco. When we arrived home later that day, Noora tried to pin the blame on me. She had confided in me, and I knew she trusted me but at the end of the day, she was still Noora! And that meant trouble! The little voice inside me told me, "Just keep quiet." I did. The 'uncle' in me and the Almost-man teamed up and decided to be patient and not react. I stood a little straighter.

"Look Aunty! Ali and I went downstairs. We had skipped breakfast."

That was true but we only skipped it because she refused to eat any of it!

"I wanted to go out and Ali came along."

I went with her because I was supposed to look out for her, and she never listens! I had to go.

"And downstairs, Aunty, Ali had the car keys in his jacket pocket, so I took them and drove the car. After all, car and keys and me. It means drive the car!"

Whoa! Hang on a minute. There were other steps to this process! She missed huge chunks of the story! I glanced over at Aunty Nelly. She was sitting relaxed and quiet with a little smile. She was being patient. I knew it.

"I was so careful driving Aunty. I never scratched your car. At all!" Well, she wasn't careful, but she didn't scratch the car. That was true.

"The whole police and entourage thing was so scary Aunty. I know you would have told me to be careful, so I was. I was really careful."

Yeah, right.

"And Ali said *Khan al Khalini* is a tourist hot spot, so I wanted to go there. It was his idea."

Liar!

"And I wanted to buy you a nice present, so I thought of an idea to get some money without doing anything, well, wrong."

She opened her eyes wide trying to look innocent. I could see that Aunty knew better but she was still quiet.

"Sorry I didn't get to give you a present Aunty. I really wanted to, but Ali insisted that he wanted to talk. I guess he has things to offload."

Almost-man inside of me wanted to jump up and take action on her lies and twisting of the truth. But the little voice inside me and my 'uncle' part had to restrain him. Eventually he calmed down.

"Never mind Lassie. All's well that ends well." Aunty was nodding her head as she spoke.

What? It hasn't ended yet! And all is definitely not well! I was boiling but decided to take Aunty's cues. There must be something else going on. I know that Aunty would never be tricked by Noora. She had been open with me, but she was still Noora.

CHAPTER 20

A Baby Boom

Aunty Nelly has lived in Egypt for many years and has made loads of friends. But there is one special friend that stands out from all the rest.

Her name is Hafsa, and she also converted to Islam a long time ago. Aunty loves to tell the story of Hafsa.

"Ach Laddie! Aunty Hafsa is an amazing lady. She has always looked out for me and accepted me for who I am."

Who wouldn't accept Aunty for who she is? Anyway.

"Aunty Hafsa married an Egyptian gentleman, but they couldn't have children and Hafsa really wanted to have a wee one. She finally convinced her husband that they should adopt a little wee girrrl."

Now there is a story behind all this. There are orphanages in Egypt. Lots of them. Some run by the government and some are privately operated. The thing is, that they are mainly filled with boys. I remember asking Aunty Nelly where all the girls were, and she didn't tell me the truth for some time. The subject saddened her greatly.

"Unfortunately, Lad, people often adopt little wee girrrls to use them as servants in their houses. Sad but true."

"What the...?" I said aloud.

When Aunty Hafsa found out about this practice, she was determined to adopt a little girl and raise her well and give her every possible opportunity.

Time passed and she and her husband went to an orphanage and were told to 'take their pick'. Tiny, helpless babies wrapped up in warm blankets in small cribs lined the walls of the dormitory. The women who cared for them were kind and loving but they had no power to reject an offer of adoption, even though they might know the terrible intention.

Aunty Hafsa and her husband were different from most people who came to adopt. There was something genuine and caring about them. The lady in charge was very pleased to meet Aunty Hafsa and asked her which baby she wanted, and Aunty couldn't choose. It sounded like she was selling shoes or a nice coat. Finally, Aunty Hafsa said, "Show me the smallest, darkest, weakest one that no one else would want."

Let me explain. In Egypt (and many other countries) fair skin colour is favoured. People here might say that isn't true, but it is, and the orphanage lady knew it and Aunty Hafsa knew it too. So, Lady in Charge showed Aunty an undersized baby who looked weak and fretful.

"She was brought to us quite late," said Lady in Charge. "But with care, the doctor says she should be fine. She is a strong little thing."

Aunty Hafsa picked her up gently and cradled her in her arms. Tears flowed, as was expected.

"What's her name?"

"Warda," said Lady in Charge with a wistful look.

Warda means flower. Nice. Papers were signed and they took baby Warda home to start her new life. That was years and years ago. Now baby Warda is teenage Warda and has become something of a challenge to her doting 'parents'.

CHAPTER 21

Warda

Warda had gone to a private school in Cairo. She was fed healthy food, taught, loved, and taken places. She had every opportunity they could give her. She even got to travel to France many times to see Aunty Hafsa's family. But there was one thing her devoted parents could not give her and that was her identity.

It is difficult to keep things hidden in Egypt; secrets always come out. The kids at school came to know that Warda was an orphan. It didn't matter that her adoptive father was a well-off engineer or that her adoptive mother was amazing. It didn't matter that Warda wore fashionable, quality clothes and shoes and had a bike, and all the toys and things that kids want. All they saw was the 'orphan' in Warda and they didn't let her forget it during all the twelve years of schooling.

Aunty Hafsa and her husband had told Warda from the start that she was adopted and that they had 'chosen' her because she was special, and they loved her instantly. She was one week old when she came to live with them.

As she grew up, Warda felt more and more alienated. She felt that she didn't belong anywhere, and she started to give Aunty Hafsa a hard time. Sometimes she would run away and stay alone all night in some deserted shed. She always came home but she punished Aunty Hafsa with her attitude and meanness. Maybe she was punishing her because she couldn't punish her biological parents. Perhaps there were times when Aunty Hafsa regretted her decision to adopt Warda, but she never let on. Her love for Warda seemed unconditional and genuine.

Somewhere along the line, Warda and Noora hooked up. We are all about the same age and had known each other since we were kids. This is what happened.

I was still on guard duty. I was supposed to stay close to Noora and 'be' there for her. I wasn't quite sure what that meant. With everything that had happened, my 'being' there didn't usually make much of a difference. Or so I thought.

We were an odd group. Me, Noora and Warda. Noora and I were a couple of tallish, frizzy red heads with freckles, and Warda was medium height, medium build with medium length brown hair. She reminded me a lot of Aunty Nelly; she didn't stand out in the crowd but on closer look, there was an energy emanating from her. Determination, a sense of humour, a natural wariness and love all rolled into one. She loved animals, plants, bugs, little kids, the sky, and books. She was very selective of adult people. They tended to hurt her. But when she peered over that wall, which she had built around herself, she could be lively and friendly. On this occasion, she had jumped over her 'wall' and was ready to engage with anyone. You see, she was on a quest. A quest to find out who she was. Once and for all.

"Oh! But you're a sweet little flower, Warda!" Noora teased.

"But 'No ra' some flowers are carnivores! I'm one of them," Warda teased back.

She insisted on calling Noora – No ra – as in No! because Noora says No! a lot and 'ra' because she tends to go on and on and on about things. They were a match. This tended to irritate Noora, so I came to like Warda more and more and, in a debate, I generally sided with her.

"You're not so sweet Warda," insisted Noora. "Your parents give you everything and think you're wonderful. What's your problem? Why are you hurting them like this?"

"I told you, I'm a carnivore! I'm looking out for me. I'm not hurting them. I care about them, but the truth is the truth. They are not my 'parents'. They are people who raised me and I'm grateful to them, but I want to know who my biological parents are. I need to know."

I nodded. I got that. Why didn't Noora get it?

"I hope you don't eat me," said Noora, "since you're a carnivore!"

"You're safe 'No Ra'! I don't like white meat!"

We laughed.

"You know they don't keep records very well here

in Egypt, Warda," said Noora. "How can you possibly find out?"

"I know the area I was brought to the orphanage from. Near Tanta. It's a smallish area and people usually know everything about everyone. Surely, someone remembers something. I'm going there and I'll ask around. If you don't want to come, don't! I can go by myself."

Almost-man inside of me stood up and said, "No! She can't go alone! Too dangerous!"

"It's too dangerous," I said. "You can't go alone."

I said it slowly and clearly. No sarcasm. Just matter of fact. They both turned to me.

"I don't need your help Ali," said Warda. "I can take care of myself. I know Arabic and Egypt way more than you."

"Maybe. But you don't have my dashing good looks or charm. I'm indispensable on a trip like this." I was grinning. She couldn't help but smile. I was not what you would call 'good looking' but I know I have charm.

"Whatever," said the little voice inside me.

"And me! Hello people! I'm coming too. Neither of you is as creative as me when it comes to 'managing' situations," stated Noora. She looked smug.

All I could think of was the car and the entourage and Burly Policeman flying from his motorbike and us escaping and her fake begging and then being found.

"You're a nightmare Noora. You should stay home and learn to cook." Warda laughed. Noora lunged at me, but I dodged, and she hit the wall and fell to the ground.

"Oh, not just good looking and charming but pretty agile too. I know how to dodge a bullet!" I added.

Warda helped Noora up and sat her down.

"Okay you two can come, but only if you let me take the lead," said Warda. "This is my thing, not yours. You - Ali - are there for decoration it seems and you No Ra are there for, well, hmm, moral support?"

The next morning, we tiptoed out the door. Aunty was still asleep – or so we thought. Noora reached for the car keys, and I pushed her out the front door before she could grab them. I checked I had my phone. Yes, Aunty had bought me a phone after the last 'Noora debacle' – that was a plus. And my wallet and house key. Good. Set to go. Almost-man inside of me, nodded proudly.

CHAPTER 22

The Journey

Begins

We got on the bus to Tanta from the top of Muqattum in the middle of Cairo. Don't ask me how we got there! Noora said she knew the way but got us on the wrong bus. We had to go the long way around. The thing is, Muqattum is a mountain, or maybe a hill. Anyway, it's rocky, steep, and dangerous. Did I mention it's dangerous? There are no guard rails on the side of the road as it twists and winds down its steep path. And I'm sure the bus driver had a death wish. The road is narrow and sandy with gravel. Perfect for skidding! The bus was hurtling along at breakneck speed. The driver was smoking a cigarette and fiddling with the radio while he navigated potentially deadly curves in the road. I have never prayed as much as I did when riding that bus! It was crowded and I had to give up my seat to an old man. I mean, no one forced me. No one said anything. I just knew that was what I was supposed to do. And I did.

Noora looked brave until she saw a high-ranking army officer nearly wrapping himself around a pole, holding on for dear life and shouting at the bus driver to slow down. He was terrified. The driver had a sense of humour. Despite my fears, I giggled.

The driver kept saying, "I can't hear. What did you say?"

I mean, the whole bus heard what the army officer was saying. Good one.

Warda was lost in thought and was totally unaware of her surroundings. She was in some other place in her mind. Lucky her.

CHAPTER 23

Tanta

The bus ride to the Tanta area was bumpy but picturesque. Green fields. Cows. Sheep. Palm trees. Nice. People strolled along, relaxed and chilled out. Not rushing and pushing and shoving like in the big city. We chatted and slept. Warda was excited like I'd never seen her before. She was total positivity. What could go wrong?

"Let's just check in at the police station first," said

Warda with confidence. She marched ahead towards a drab looking building, wedged between two newly built houses. Noora and I followed behind in humble obedience. This was her day.

Noora was always putting a plan B in place and today was no different. Her survival mode continually run on high alert.

"Just remember," said Noora. "If there is any trouble, you are deaf Warda, and Ali and I don't speak any Arabic. We will look dumb." She nodded as she spoke. Speak for yourself!

The police officer smiled when he saw Noora and I. We were fair-skinned foreigners after all. I started to hate my light, freckly skin. I hated that he ignored Warda. I hated that he made a difference between us. I hated it especially because of what Warda was trying to achieve that day.

She wanted information to prove that she belonged to these people and here she was, being overlooked. I wished I could wrap her in cotton wool and protect her from what's out there. All the pain and hurt. Getting abused and being under-valued. My face had taken on a more serious look generally. Almost-man was flexing his muscles. The little voice inside me said, "Just pray."

Helpful Policeman spoke in English even though Warda was rattling away in Arabic. I could see he wanted to impress me and Noora.

I must admit something before I proceed with this part of the story. Aunty Nelly had let me in on a well-guarded secret. I was under strict instructions to be surprised if I ever found out. But she said she respected me enough to tell me the truth, especially as I was to accompany the girls that day. Yes, she knew what we were up to. Spoiler alert. There will be more tears. Such was my life that I had taken to carrying tissues with me in my pocket.

There are different kinds of orphanages in Egypt. One is for children whose parents are known and who died. The other is for children whose parents are unknown. The children in the former are considered 'respectable' and the orphans receive special treatment. The children in the latter are branded 'illegitimate' and are subjected to sub-standard treatment. I mean they are clothed and fed and educated but they will not have access to the same opportunities or good treatment.

I had previously gone with Aunty Nelly to see an

orphanage that had just opened. It was founded and funded by a wealthy, well-known figure in the Middle East. Aunty Nelly asked him straight up about the status of 'illegitimate' orphans and his response was far from Islamic. He actually used the word 'dirty' when describing the children. Aunty had grabbed me by the arm and marched us out of the place. That is, of course, after she gave him – and all the important people there that day – a lecture.

She stood as tall and straight as she could in their midst and talked about the dignity of human beings in Islam, the example of the Prophet (peace be upon him) when dealing with orphans and how far away we are from calling ourselves 'Muslims'! She was loud and clear. Not aggressive. But in a few concise words put everyone in their place. I wish I could have been a fly on the wall to hear their reactions after she and I left but I will have to make do with imagining. She said she would have nothing to do with treating innocent children differently because of the circumstances surrounding their birth! Go Aunty!

Abandoned babies are found all the time in Egypt. Some are found in *masjids,* wrapped up lovingly and abandoned. Some in shop entrances or bathrooms. All kinds of places. All kinds of circumstances.

It so happened that a man was walking to work one day and was passing by a vacant lot. He heard a mewing sound. At first, he thought it was a cat, but something made him stop and listen more carefully. He walked through the garbage that was strewn across the empty land, following the sound. It was the local dumping ground where people flung their rubbish bags. At last, he came to the source of the sound and reached down, rummaging through old newspapers and rotting trash. He uncovered a baby. A small, squirming baby girl. He quickly took off his expensive jacket and wrapped the infant in it, holding her firmly but gently in his strong arms. He hurried away with her and went to the nearest police station. The baby was taken from him and given a name and a number that were recorded in a big, black book. The man left. I have no way of knowing how he felt or what he was thinking. He did a good deed. He was responsible. He saved a life. He saved Warda's life.

CHAPTER 24

From One to Another

Helpful Police Officer was talkative and friendly. Very different from Burly Police Officer on the motorbike! Maybe it's another difference between city and country people.

"I'm looking for my parents," announced Warda.

Now that she was confronted with the reality of what she was searching for, I could see that she felt awkward and unsure of herself.

"Where do they live?" asked Helpful Policeman.

I interjected. Almost-man inside of me wanted to shield Warda. I had no idea how Helpful Policeman would react to her.

"They died a long time ago. She doesn't know who they are. We are here to find out," I said, looking him in the eye. Man to almost-man. He nodded. Warda looked at me appreciatively. She looked small in that gloomy, crowded police station.

He paused for a moment, staring at an ink spot on the desk.

"I see," was his reply.

He paused again, then went to an adjoining room and closed the door. We could hear him talking in hushed whispers to another officer. Soon he returned.

"I assume you were in an orphanage." He spoke directly to Warda.

She nodded.

"Which orphanage was that?" he asked Warda. He couldn't maintain eye contact with her. You could cut the air with a knife.

She told him. Helpful Policeman looked down again. He was silent. Now I knew and he knew what that meant. It meant that Warda had been abandoned and was considered illegitimate. There was absolutely no way anyone would know who her parents were or who abandoned her and why. He didn't have the heart to tell her.

That day, I learnt the value of beating around the bush. I discovered that the Egyptian people are really good at it. Sometimes it is annoying but at other times it hits the target; it is exactly what is needed.

"Do you know your family name?" he inquired, looking at her.

Warda shook her head. She looked helpless.

Helpful Policeman was about forty years old. He had a big, round belly and trim moustache. He wore a wedding band and probably had children of his own. He looked at Warda and sighed. The father in him wanted to reach out and make things better.

He pointed a friendly finger at her and said, "You know, you look like someone I used to know a long time ago. You might be related. Why not go to the coffee shop down the street and ask for *Hagga* Mahmoud. Tell him I sent you."

I looked again at Helpful Policeman. He didn't realize how important he was in this sensitive situation.

He put his head down with a mixture of shame and sadness. This was his country after all, and these were his people. I appreciated his kindness towards Warda. But at the same time, I knew he was enabling a wild goose chase. But then so was I. What else could he – we – do? The truth would be way too painful for her. She honestly thought her parents' identity had been lost in bungling paperwork. There was nothing else I could do but stand by her and try to catch her if she fell. He managed to smile warmly as we prepared to leave. He made *Duaa* for us and nodded again. I gathered my things and started to follow the girls up the street to meet *Hagga* Mahmoud. But before I left the police station, I turned to Helpful Policeman and quietly said, "*Shukran*". He smiled.

CHAPTER 25

Coffee Shop and Beyond

After we left the dingy police station and trekked through the dusty street to find *Hagga* Mahmoud, Warda had a little spring in her step again. She stopped when she saw a little girl, alone, playing in the dirt. Her light brown hair was matted, her face was grimy, and her clothes were ragged but when she saw Warda she smiled.

An open, genuine, joyful smile.

Warda squatted beside her and spoke to her. They giggled and then Warda gave her some money and pointed to the nearby bakery. The little girl raced off with a grateful nod. Warda watched her running happily to buy some food. She was lost in thought. A look of pity and curiosity. She sincerely believed that her family roots were in this place, so when she encountered any person, she wondered if they were related.

Noora was starting to look bored. I was afraid she would seek out some more adventure that would only lead to trouble. I was trying not to panic.

Warda approached the waiter at the local coffee shop Helpful Policeman had mentioned and asked for *Hagga* Mahmoud. Noora and I stayed in the background.

Men crowded the small tables and chairs. They were served steamy hot tea in tiny glasses and strong bitter coffee in small dainty cups. Many played backgammon or cards. The air was thick with cigarette smoke and *shisha*.

I didn't feel Noora or Warda were entirely safe in that place, and I tried to place myself between the men and Noora while Warda spoke to the waiter.

"What are you doing Ali McDougal? I can't see what's going on."

"Nothing is going on here. Just a bunch of men smoking and drinking coffee. We will be done soon. I can hardly breathe."

That was true. The smoky air was tickling my throat and I was trying to resist about of coughing. That's when Noora started to sneeze. Not a small, dainty sneeze. But a loud, rambunctious sneeze that threatened to shake the entire building!

"What the…." I said incredulously. "What was that? An earthquake?"

Everyone in the coffee shop stopped what they were doing and looked directly at Noora. She looked embarrassed and sniffed.

"Looks like I'm allergic to something."

I took that as an excuse to get her out of there. I hustled her out the door and handed her a tissue. She smiled thankfully.

"What a sleazy place," she commented.

At last, we agreed on something.

Warda soon approached us with a beaming smile.

"I got an address!" she cried, waving a torn off

piece of paper in her hand with a scribbled address written in Arabic.

"Cool," I said. "Whose address is that?"

"Well," said Warda. "*Hagga* Mahmoud said I might be related to his relatives' friend, and they live on a farm not very far from here."

"His relatives' friend?" I queried. She was grasping at straws.

"That's what he said," she said innocently. "Are you guys okay to come with me? You don't have to. I'm good to go alone."

"No, no. All good. We are coming with you." Noora nodded. She looked restless.

"Yeah, I feel like some action," Noora announced.

Warda and I looked at each other. We knew what that meant.

"You have to behave yourself 'No Ra'!" said Warda firmly. "Today is about me, remember. I don't want you to ruin it."

No begging 'No Ra'!" I mimicked. "No driving cars! No knocking policemen off their motorbikes!" I added.

We all chuckled.

"Let it go," said Noora. "You don't have to drag up the past all the time."

"Let's just go," begged Warda. She was in a hurry to discover who she really was and who she belonged to.

CHAPTER 26

Sharpen Your Elbows!

We had to catch yet another bus. As we approached the bus station, I saw how crowded it was. The difference between this bus station and those in Cairo is that here there were not only people boarding the buses, but people with chickens, people with baskets of vegetables precariously balanced on well-trained heads, and I also saw a goat being carried on a man's shoulders. So, the sights and smells were unique, to say the least. My heart sank as I wondered how I could possibly navigate all this.

To top it all off, my spoken Arabic was pitiful. I could recite *Quran* but I was out of my league with everyday chit chat! Even when I said 'excuse me' in colloquial Arabic, it sounded Weird. Warda said I sounded like someone trying to speak English and saying things like, "please, me excuse" instead of 'excuse me please'. Or, 'that I want very much thank you please'. My argument is that the people always got me what I wanted; they seemed to understand me! But her criticisms had chipped away at my self-confidence and now I only spoke when I really had to. Today was one of those days. I think my story of today's 'bus encounter' has gone down in Tanta history. After what happened, I think I might actually be a legend!

Warda was forging her way forward towards the door of the bus. Noora trailed closely behind her, holding tightly to her jacket. She knew instinctively that she was better off with Warda than with me in such situations. I was left behind. I couldn't believe how fast they moved and weaved their way through the crowds of people.

There were about five people between me and the door of the bus and other people kept pushing in. The Aussie in me wanted to be polite and let them on first and wait my turn. Warda and Noora were staring at me from inside the bus and giggling. They even managed to get a seat! I waited for the other people to board but then more people pushed past me and flung me aside and climbed onto the bus. I was continually left standing there, looking confused and feeling helpless.

"What the...?" I was speechless. That's not fair. Almost-man inside me flexed his muscles and rolled up his sleeves. Not a bad idea!

Now, despite the few words I knew in colloquial Arabic, my mind went blank with all the commotion, dust, noise, and pushiness. Polite phrases and words disappeared from my short-term memory, and I was left with the odd word that dashed to and fro across my mind. I'd had enough of being pushed aside and I was worried the bus would leave without me and with the girls on board! So, I rolled up my sleeves, sharpened my elbows and started shouting '*Mish*! *Mish*'.

In my defence, I had heard the word '*Mish*' very

often when people speak. I heard it in the context of meaning 'no or not'. For example, '*mish ouz*' (I don't want). It is definitely a negative! So, to my traumatized brain it made sense to say – or rather shout – No! Not! – as I struggled and fought to get on the bus. There was, however, something I had yet to learn. When said together '*Mish Mish*' –means apricot. So here I was with rolled up sleeves, revealing my skinny freckled arms, my woollen hat pushed back, revealing my frizzy bright red curls and I'm shouting 'Apricot! Apricot!' and jostling to get on a bus.

I must have looked like an oddball and perhaps some people were afraid of me and what I might do. But somehow it worked. There was a man with a briefcase who had just pushed me out of the way and a rotund woman carrying a huge basket on her head who had sent me flying. I was picking myself up off the ground, still shouting '*Mish! Mish!*' and they both stopped. Looked at me. Looked at each other and shook their heads. Then they moved aside and ushered me politely onto the bus as if I was a celebrity or something. There was a hush. No one in the crowd around the bus spoke or moved for a short time. I looked around me. All eyes were on me.

The farmers, the workers, the businessmen, the women, the children were all looking at me. Did I mention the chickens and the goat? They stared at me too! There was no expression on their faces. Just silent stares. At that moment, I wasn't sure what had created the momentous change in my circumstances. But I didn't stop to find out. With as much dignity as I could muster, I nodded politely to the man with the briefcase and the woman with the basket and boarded the bus.

Noora and Warda were in fits of laughter. They were both crying uncontrollably and laughing convulsively.

"What's so funny? I don't see what the joke is," I said rather grimly. Almost-man was seriously embarrassed. They started again.

"You are definitely a weirdo Ali McDougal! Apricot! Apricot," mimicked Warda.

She was almost choking on her laughter. Almost-man, with a mortified expression, definite frown, and half-closed eyes looked coldly and said, "Not funny."

I became more and more serious, the more they laughed. Then I noticed people on the bus looking at me and smiling. The bus had started to move. That's when

Warda informed me of my mistake.

"You were shouting 'Apricot! Apricot!' and trying to get on the bus. *Mish mish* means apricot Ali!" They both roared with laughter again and I felt shock-waves bouncing through me. It was worse than I thought.

"Liar!" I replied defensively.

A few people on the bus spoke English and everyone was listening to us. Two people nodded and said, "Yes, that's right. '*Mish mish*' means apricot." They chuckled too.

"Your turn will come," I threatened the girls. But I felt like an idiot. The little voice inside me was doubled up laughing. Almost-man wanted to knock him out.

CHAPTER 27

Tant Faatima

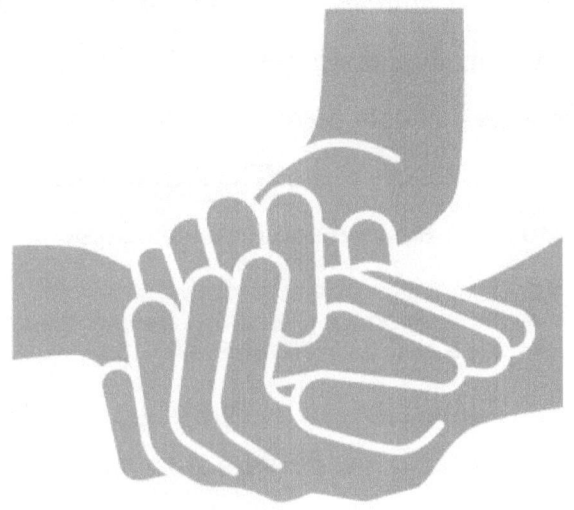

The bus let us down just up the road from a farm that was owned by *Hagga* Mahmoud's cousin, *Hagga* Mustafa and his wife Faatima. Obviously, many phone calls had been made between the time we visited the police station until we emerged from the bus. They were waiting for us and welcomed us like long-lost relatives.

Hagga Mustafa and his wife Faatima had eight children. Some were married and living on the farm with their families so there were crowds of people and multitudes of kids running barefoot through the fields.

They enveloped us with hugs and shook hands vigorously. I had never seen such happy, carefree kids. A part of me felt a little jealous. Instinctively I started to race with them and playfully threw the little ones in the air. Of course, I caught them. All to the joy and amazement of *Tant* Faatima. The kids wanted to touch my hair to see if it was real. Gentle and some not-so-gentle pulls and tugs. Yes, it's real!

Noora and Warda were scooped up in warm bear hugs by *Tant* Faatima. *Tant* means 'aunty' and is used to show respect even to people who are not relatives. But she behaved like a relative that day. A loving, caring, gushing Aunty! She, and her husband, could speak simple English and so could most of the children. I entered the house holding two of the younger ones who refused to let me go. It was kind of nice.

The house was made from mud brick. It was simple and practical. Chickens, ducks, and geese wandered around the garden and sometimes rambled into the house, just to be shooed out. There were dogs and many cats close to the house. Tall trees shielded the home from the hot sun and the fields beyond were a lush green. There were cows and buffalo. I could also see horses in a nearby field and sheep. The horses were not majestic like the ones I rode with General Ghuraab, but they enriched the look of the place. I love horses.

The furniture in the living room was simple. The place had been swept clean. There were wooden floorboards and the tables, and the shelves had plastic flowers in vases with hand crafted doilies. We were invited to sit down on the couch and the children sat on the floor quietly and watched us. I noticed how well-behaved the children were. *Tant* Faatima only had to look at them and they sat quietly. She fussed around us and served us tea, as well as oranges that she cut up in front of us and offered us with her hand. She chatted away and made us feel welcome and loved.

Then I started to feel an itch. I casually rubbed my leg. Then I scratched my ankle with my other foot. Finally, I scratched my chin. My hair. I looked at the girls. Noora was scratching her leg. I tried so hard to ignore the itch, but I couldn't help it. Then I saw it. A flea cheekily jumped onto my arm, and I automatically smacked it out of existence. It was a loud smack. Everyone looked at me. The girls looked mortified. The kids giggled. I smiled politely and pretended I was doing a drum roll. I successfully turned my flea smacking into a musical gig. The kids roared with laughter and copied me. Everyone relaxed. I shifted in my seat a bit hoping the flea I swiped didn't have any friends hanging around.

Noora nudged me and whispered, "It's a farm, you know Ali McDougal. Mud bricks and animals everywhere. Of course, there will be fleas!" She scratched her head again, as if to prove her point.

I ignored her. Warda was in raptures with *Tant* Faatima and didn't notice the flea episode at all.

Thankfully we were soon invited into the dining room where *Tant* Faatima had cooked up a feast. I was starving. The girls were starving. Now, I'm not a fussy eater and neither is Noora but one thing we don't and won't eat is liver. There is no amount of money or bribe that will induce either of us to consume organ meat. Guess what *Tant* Faatima was serving that day? The biggest platter of fried liver I had ever seen or could have imagined. Noora and I looked at each other and tried to smile. Our hearts sank. Did I mention that we were starving? Warda looked happy. She liked fried liver. She had a big job ahead of her that day.

Tant Faatima was bustling from the kitchen to the dining room. She was wearing a long black dress with a colourful apron. Her hair was tied up in a coloured bandana wrapped around her head. She wore well-worn sandals. Although she was short and round, she moved fast and chatted endlessly. She was like a whirlwind of energy. She chased the children away so we could eat in peace. But I saw their little faces looking through the window, watching our every move. They would have a lot to report later.

Tant Faatima heaped freshly cooked rice, tasty salad, and mountains of liver onto our plates. We nodded politely and said '*shukran*'. Then she left the room to prepare the men's food. The children would take it to them in the fields.

"Warda, you're going to have to eat this," I demanded in a whisper, as I proceeded to transfer my liver onto her plate.

"And mine," said Noora, as she did the same.

"Hang on, you guys. I can't possibly eat all that!"

"Warda! If I put it in my mouth, I'll barf all over the place. Now you don't want that to happen, right?"

Noora nodded her head in agreement.

"I knew I should have come alone," grumbled Warda.

She scoffed down as much liver as she could, so that when *Tant* Faatima entered the room she was satisfied that we were eating.

"Oh good! You like *kibda,*" said *Tant* Faatima. She piled our plates up with more and disappeared again into the kitchen.

I wanted to escape but I knew I was trapped. I would do anything to help Warda, but I wouldn't eat liver for her. I was at a loss. Noora and I continued to put our liver onto Warda's plate, and she was now full and couldn't eat another thing, so she was putting the liver back onto the platter. So, when *Tant* Faatima returned to the room, we were all eating and saying we were full, but the platter looked very much the same as it had done in the beginning. The kind lady scratched her head, feeling confused. Then she smiled and trotted back to the kitchen. This time she brought out a huge ceramic pot with clear broth and an animal floating in it.

Warda leaned over and whispered, "It's a goose."

I gulped. Noora stared at its head and little beady eyes. We froze. Goose soup was immediately added to our list of foods we won't eat. It came in second, just after fried liver. *Tant* Faatima dished us up large pieces of goose meat, more rice and *molokhia*, which is a thick, green soup. It tasted really nice, but nothing could induce me to eat the goose. None of us wanted to hurt *Tant* Faatima's feelings but we didn't know how to escape this. Then we were saved.

There was a ruckus outside. Stomping of feet. Loud voices and bellowing laughter. The men were coming. The children hovered around them and were picked up, joked with, and then turned out as they entered the house. They removed their sandals at the door and settled in the living room. The three of us jumped up, said *'shukran'* many times to *Tant* Faatima and headed to the living room to join them.

Hagga Mahmoud took the lead and spoke in Arabic and in English where he could. After the initial chit chat, he gestured to the other men to leave, and they did. Soon it was just me and the girls and *Tant* Faatima and her husband.

Hagga Mahmoud smiled gently and looked at
Warda who beamed back. This was her hope, her chance.

"Ya Faatima!" he exclaimed to his wife. "Warda
looks like that lady we knew – a long time ago – Sanaya.
Yes, Sanaya. I remember her. The one who lived near the
river. Do you remember her?"

"Yes. Yes. I remember Sanaya. She and her
husband, um, weren't they in a car accident?"

"I believe they were. So sad. Both of them died in
the accident."

They both sat, sadly shaking their heads.

"Such nice people," stated *Tant* Faatima.

They were good. I started to believe them myself. I
know it was all made up for the benefit of Warda, but
wow! I was impressed.

"And Sanaya had the same hands as Warda. I
remember," added *Tant* Faatima.

They proceeded to tell stories about these fictitious
people's days at school and the work they did and how
well-liked they were. *Tant* Faatima got up and sat next to
Warda and picked up her hand gently and held it.

"Yes, the same hands. The same kind face," said
Tant Faatima with great warmth. She leaned over and

hugged Warda as if she were her own child. The kind lady had tears in her eyes as she fussed over Warda.

"What a beautiful girl, *Mashallah*!" she announced. She looked at Noora and I kindly.

"You are lucky to have Warda as your friends. Sanaya and her husband were very good people."

I found myself imagining Sanaya and her husband. I got completely carried away by the narrative. Noora had tears in her eyes as she saw the look of contentment on Warda's face.

"It's a pity they don't keep good records here in Egypt," said *Hagga* Mahmoud. He shook his head, disappointedly.

He pointed to his chest, then waved his hands and said, "My country – Egypt – is not very organized. I'm sorry."

Then he turned to Warda. "But you dear girl are a lovely girl. So, blessed. You have very good friends. You are welcome here any time," he said quietly.

Tant Faatima continued to sit next to Warda and hug her and say kind things to her until Warda relaxed and it was time to go.

When we started this venture, I had no idea how it would play out. But I could never have imagined it would be like this. So much kindness. Sincerity. Warmth. Compassion for a young orphan girl who wanted to know who she is. But who never would. One thing for sure, Warda is Egyptian and if she has half the kindness and decency of the people we met that day, she is truly blessed to be one of them. I was a changed person. The little voice inside of me said, "Ali. You're growing up." I nodded.

As we prepared to leave their home, I looked at *Hagga* Mahmoud with deep respect. Their story was totally made up. But it was done with genuine love and kindness. Perhaps it is better to get through your growing up years with a pleasant fantasy. The little voice inside me agreed and said, "She will understand it all herself one day." I agreed.

I looked at Warda and thought about all she had done that day. Courage – your name is Warda.

※

We walked up the trail leading to the bus stop. *Hagga* Mahmoud was busily talking about his farm and the animals. We were sorry to leave. Then I heard quick footsteps rushing behind us and I turned to see *Tant* Faatima quickly approaching us. We stopped.

"Don't go yet. I have something for you to eat on the bus. It's a long way home," she called. Cows in the nearby field stopped munching grass and looked at us. If they had known what was in the container they would have run for their lives.

She had packed up a container filled to the brim with rice and fried liver. She handed it to me, and I thanked her profusely then I handed it to Warda.

"This is for you."

I wondered how much of all that story Warda had believed. Was she convinced that Sanaya and her husband were her parents? She was very quiet on the bus ride home. She sat and stared out of the window and Noora and I gave her space. I didn't feel like talking either.

Warda's situation made me think about my own. My parents were on the other side of the world. To be honest, I didn't think about them often. My life in Egypt was so full and busy, that days went past without me sending a text message or an email. I had this nagging feeling that I had been ungrateful. It was a new feeling, and I wasn't quite sure what to do with it. So, I quietly thanked Allah, for everything. I meant it. Everything that led me to that day on the bus and the realization of how fortunate and blessed I was, appeared to my mind like a rocky road full of twists and turns. Difficult to navigate. Painful at times. But it led me to where I am today. I had the dawning realization that if it wasn't for second chances, we would all be alone.

CHAPTER 28

Dad

We had been home for several days. Same old routine. I had my online school. Noora was being tutored by Aunty Nelly and Warda was just hanging out with us. I was finding it difficult to settle into my work routine. Things just felt different since 'Warda's day', as we called it. Aunty Nelly heard all about it from Warda and then privately I told her the story from my point of view. We were both concerned how Warda would understand what she had been told and how it would impact her.

We decided to keep our eyes on her and keep her close. She didn't want to go home yet, and no one pushed her. But I was restless and unsettled. I remembered the annoying flea that ended its life on my arm, and I believe I was bitten by the love bug. That's the only way I could account for my urge to contact my dad.

Dad! He seemed like a stranger to me. I really didn't know him. I didn't know his favourite colour or even when his birthday was. It seemed like a lifetime ago since I left Australia with my attitude and predilection for trouble. I was really a trouble magnet, like Aunty had described me. It seemed like my life had been on life support until recently. But like Aunty Nelly used to say, "Things get clearer with time." What was becoming more and more clear was the fact that I missed him. I missed my dad. Who would have thought?

CHAPTER 29

Defining Moments

Through all these adventures, all these disasters, all these learnings – Aunty was with me. I may have sneaked off from time to time, but she was there. If she wasn't physically present, her voice was in my head and my whole being leaned towards her and what she hoped and dreamed for me. It was something like a magnet, drawing me away from danger and towards, hmm.. not sure yet what I was heading towards.

Aunty described the 'heading towards' as 'discovering your path while you're on it'. That made me think. One day, Aunty asked me what the most important thing was I had learned this year. It took me two days to decide on an answer. In the beginning it was something about boiled eggs, then it moved on to justice (Burly Policeman and Shop Owner), but then it morphed into something quite surprising. It was Warda's Day that showed me my most important lesson. 'Compassion and concern'. That was my most important lesson. I mean, people do things for a reason. Then as they are walking their path, they might get to see things differently, so they head off in another direction. It's like, life is this massive adventure all on its own, even before we head out of the house.

Aunty Nelly and I had settled down into 'make Ali succeed' routine. She wasn't just aiming at my education. When I told her that she said indignantly, "Ach Laddie! You've no learrrrned anything all this time! Education gives ye a toolbox to work with in life. It is not the end goal!" She was almost screeching these words at me. Should I have known that before? Anyway. "Life happens on the inside Laddie!" She was still screeching. She pounded her chest and then gently patted mine. "Here Ali McDougal! This is where you become a good man. An honest, caring man. It starts inside ye'self."

So as these truths were dawning on me, I started to see things more differently. I was taking on a new direction in life. Noora seemed less annoying, and she was rapidly gaining strength and confidence. Under the guiding hands of Aunty, there was no other choice! But it was Warda that filled me with compassion. That caring feeling that pushes you to want to protect and support and help. I found it rather scary because there was nothing I could do really.

"She has her own path Laddie," Aunty had reassured me. "She's not alone on her path. Allah is with her. Now don't worry ye'self."

But how could I not worry?

"But Aunty!" I demanded, "Warda has this huge problem in her life. And it will never be fixed. It's like a gap or a chasm that you can't cross." I was worked up.

"And she is alone. Aunty sometimes I wander why Allah lets these things happen, like what happened to Warda." I half whispered these words. I put my head down.

Aunty sat beside me on the couch and patted my hand. "Only Allah knows the secrets of His creation, but I can make a good guess." I looked at her expectantly.

"This situation Laddie has taught you compassion, caring, kindness. It has made you see life beyond ye'self. And it has unlocked a part of your wee heart that was closed before. And that is precious. And," she added, "Warda is not alone. Allah sent you and all of us."

I knew that was true. That's when I decided to arrange a facetime call with Dad. Aunty had shown me some photos of when he was my age.

"Aunty! He looks like me or, I look like him! We could be twins but his clothes look old-fashioned. I wouldn't be found dead in that shirt!"

"Ali McDougal, that was the fashion at that time. And ye father was a handsome wee fella'." I didn't want to argue with that. Afterall, we looked so much alike!

"Is that Dad riding a horse?" I peered closely at the old photo. Then I realized. "He was in a rodeo!" Aunty smiled.

"Ach Laddie, you're such a baby sometimes. Who do you think taught you to ride? Have you forgotten?"

I had! The little voice inside me rolled its eyes. I wasn't listening much at that time of my life.

"Hang on Aunty! Is this Dad on a motorbike? Is he wearing a leather jacket? Is that a skull on it?"

Aunty snatched the photo from me and tried to tuck it under a cushion. I grabbed it back and held it up high. She rolled her eyes in resignation. Now I knew. "Dad was a bikie?"

"Laddie, that was a long time ago."

I could see that. The photo was ancient and ragged around the edges. "Who is that lady beside him?" I asked. I was intrigued. Aunty coughed nervously.

"That's ye mother."

Mum was a bikie chick!

"Laddie! That was before that embraced Islam. It was a long time ago."

"I know Aunty. I get it. I am just a bit surprised is all." I was gobsmacked. I knew I had uncovered secrets that they obviously didn't want me to know. I didn't want to get Aunty into trouble, but I wanted to work with this information.

CHAPTER 30

Facetime!

My facetime call with Dad was going well. Too well.

"Good for you son, I heard you've been studying and working hard."

"Ah yeah Dad. I'm getting the hang of it over here." Awkward pause.

"Ah Dad. I'm still trying to decide on which subjects I'll do next year, and I was thinking to take a trip to *Sharm Al Sheikh*. I've saved up quite a bit of money."

Dad nodded. He was waiting. So, I just blurted it out.

"So, Dad, I'm planning to use my money and buy a motor bike and head off into the sunset." I laughed. It was a nervous laugh. Part of me wanted his approval, part wanted to break free. I wasn't sure which part would win. It made me feel a bit uncomfortable. There was silence for what seemed like ages. I didn't look at the screen.

"Well Ali, I think that's a fantastic idea."

I nearly fell off my chair! Did Dad just say I could ride a motor bike to *Sharm Al Sheikh*?

Dad coughed nervously. I was looking at him with different eyes. He and I looked so alike at my age. Was I going to look like him when I got older? I studied his face, trying to decipher my future looks.

"When are you leaving?" he asked. "How long will you be away?"

I couldn't believe he had agreed so fast. Something was up.

"I'll be honest with you son."

He called me son!

"Aunty had a word with me about this motor bike trip and we both agreed you can go."

After the facetime call, I was stunned. I actually had to pinch myself to make sure I wasn't dreaming. I kind of floated into the living room and saw Aunty sitting on the couch reading her book.

"You talked to Dad about my motor bike trip?"

"Of course, Lad. That's a big decision to make."

"And I can go? Really?"

"Of course."

"One thing Aunty. I know how to ride a motorbike, but I don't know the way to *Sharm Al Sheikh*."

I felt a bit embarrassed, but it was true. In Egypt there were no maps as we know them.

"Ach Ali! Do ye think ye'll be going on your own?" She muttered something under her breath and shook her head.

"Ah yes," I answered.

"So ye father left it to me to tell you. Come here Lad."

She pointed to the couch. I walked obediently over to her and sat down. Everything seemed surreal.

"Now this is how it is going to be. Ye can ride yer motorbike and me, Noora and Warda will be in the car following behind ye, all the way to *Sharm Al Sheikh*. It will be fun."

I raised an eyebrow and stared at the carpet on the floor, trying to imagine the five and half hour ride with Aunty and Co rattling along behind me. It wasn't exactly the 'bikie' image I was unconsciously trying to live up to. But then, as I looked at her, I knew I had no choice in the matter. That SMS was honed in on me - again. It was a case of like it or lump it. So, I decided to like it.

"I have two conditions Aunty."

She turned towards me. "Go ahead. What are they?"

I sat up straight and said in as manly a way as I could, "I want to wear a leather jacket and I want Hany to come too. He can use his uncle's motor bike."

"Ach Ali McDougal. Ye never cease to surprise me."

She called the girls to come into the living room. It almost looked as if the whole thing was staged.

"Ta da!" Noora and Warda said in unison. They held up a very sleek, very cool leather jacket. Then they turned it around and I saw a bunch of little pink and purple skulls on the back. Just like the ones on Noora's bags I had carried at the airport ages ago.

"You want me to wear that?"

"You have to wear it, or we won't come," said Noora. "And if we won't come, Aunty can't come and if Aunty can't come, you can't go."

Nearly-man inside me wanted to pounce on her but the little voice said quietly, "All good. We'll find a way."

"Whatever," I said, with a careless gesture.

As it turned out, we had the best holiday ever! All those hours riding along the desert roads with Aunty and Co just behind me, gave me time to think back and reflect. All the lessons learnt. All the connections made and remade. And I saw it all so clearly. The people Allah had sent into my life and those He removed. The people who came and went so quickly. It all had meaning. I had to go through it all and experience it, then the understanding, the wisdom would kick in later. Even the wrong choices I made became a valuable lesson when looking back. I realized it all depended on sincerity. At the time of learning, it was like I was walking in the dark and if I was to receive guidance from Allah, I had to look inward and take notice. I had to search my soul for the answers. And the answers were always there.

This was to be our last taste of freedom and carefree happiness before the 'Arab Spring'. Hours of desert sun, and a warm breeze with me in my customized leather jacket and a car full of females with three hijabs fluttering in the breeze as they zoomed behind me in Aunty's little car. That's the year my dad came over and stayed with us. He was there, with me, when the revolution started. And he was there, with me, when it all came to an end. But that's a whole other story.

Glossary

Ach   Oh!

Ach aye   Oh yes!

Adhan   Call to prayer made five times a day

Aye   Yes

'Beat around the bush'   To discuss a matter without coming to the point.

Bonnie   Attractive or beautiful

Daft   crazy

Dah!   A playful term describing someone who did something foolish

Dunna   Do not

Fajr Prayer   Early morning Prayer before daybreak

Falafel   A vegetarian fritter

Falukha   Sailing boat

Ful beans   Broad beans

Gotcha'   Got you

Grrrand   Grand (wonderful)

Hagga   Respectful term like Mister. Also used to refer to someone who has performed pilgrimage to Makkah

Haram   Not allowed in Islam

Inshallah   Allah Willing

Juma'ah   Congregational Prayer

Kofta   A savoury meat ball.

Laddie Young man (an endearing term)
La hawla wa la quwatta illah billah There is no power or strength except by Allah the Almighty, the Great.
Lassie Young lady
Masjid Mosque
Pet an endearing term, like, 'dear'.
Quran Sacred Book of the Muslims
Shisha A tobacco pipe with a long flexible tube that draws tobacco smoke through water contained in a bowl. It can also be flavoured, for example, with mint
Shukran Thank you
'sick dunk' An amazing goal
Thowb Long garment worn by men.
Ye You
Yer Your
YOLO 'You only live one' . Said when someone is trying to be tough while taking a risk.
Wee Small, little

Other Books by
Selma Cook
Amirah Stevenson Series

Buried Treasure

The Colour of Fear